The Piano

by

Carol M. Blackford

For Terry

Contents

Introduction

Many seasons have come and gone. Forgive me, but
I seem to have lost track of time. You see, I'm rather old
and have been alone for many years. People don't visit me
here anymore. They are all too busy with other things. My
family moved away and left me. Perhaps I had become too
much of a burden. I'm not sure. They placed me in the care
of others who often mistreated me and there was nothing
I could do. It's been horrible waiting for someone to show
some concern. How I long to be loved, wanted and needed
just once more. Why am I still here? My family may have
forgotten about me, but I have not forgotten about them.

It's dark where I sit each day and night. It's often
too hot or too cold. It certainly not a pleasant room. I
remember brightly colored rooms filled with sunshine and
activity. Now just a sliver of sunshine can filter through
the broken boards and leaky roof. I hear the booming
of thunder and torrents of rain pelting when it storms.
Sometimes the wind roars and whistles through this
ramshackle building making frightening sounds. I wouldn't
mind the dreadful commotion nearly so much if I wasn't
so alone. Bird songs still have a way of cheering my long

days. Oh, but I would much rather hear the laughter of a child or someone humming alongside me though. Nothing was more wonderful than to be included in their lives. I remember their love and caresses. Now, I feel discarded and unloved. I miss playing my music and performing more than words can express. They used to say I was quite extraordinary. However, that was ages ago when I was young and rather beautiful. People came from all around just to admire my fine looks and listen to me play. My family was proud of me then. Maybe someday they will come back to take me home. I hope so. Until then, I will just sit, wait and listen.

♫ ♫ ♫

Black Hills, 1956

Mark Kinney was an objective, analytical man until he walked through the old gold mining town of Credence. An engineer in World War II, he knew how to build roads and bridges as well as destroy them. He was contracted by the Bureau of Reclamation to oversee a project in the Black Hills of South Dakota, the flooding of Credence. He never questioned the decisions of flooding vast western lands for water use. He simply followed orders and met deadlines.

However, there was something about the sweeping landscape of this place that caught him unaware. Its beauty made him question the wisdom of flooding it. He was caught with the sound of water babbling in the nearby stream and cool wind rushing through the black canyon. They were alive with voices of brave souls who once made their home on the ground he stood upon. He felt something or someone was watching him, but it was only the shadow of the tall ponderosa. With each step he took, he was transfixed and transported back in time. His mind dwelled upon those who lived, laughed and loved in the decaying town. A stubborn few remained in the little settlement until mining profits dwindled. Although it was the town's death sentence, they decided to stay and were buried nearby. Mark knew all that remained of Credence along with its memories, would soon be drowned under a massive reservoir.

After a few minutes he stopped in front of a two-story wooden building. It reminded him of a battle-worn sentry unwilling to give up the battle even though it was long lost. The dilapidated frame building still bore its name in faded letters, The Nugget.

It would be hours before his crew arrived to demolish the buildings. Mark went back to his truck to get a crowbar, leather gloves and flashlight. Something about the old saloon drew him in.

It wasn't long before the weathered boards were torn away allowing sunshine to filter in and access to the building. With the sun at his back, he stepped inside. Except for a thick layer of dust, the room looked eerily intact. Tables and chairs were neatly arranged, glasses unbroken and bottles still corked as if waiting for customers. It was an unusual and strange sight. Oddly, the other structures in the ghost town had already collapsed, victims of time and nature. But not this one. In his experience abandoned buildings were always left in tatters either by mother nature or mankind. Sadly, some were even vandalized by malicious or ignorant people. He smiled thinking the old building really was a sentry.

He glimpsed his reflection in the old mirror that hung behind the bar. How did it manage to survive he wondered? It was amazing. He dusted off the bar top with his sleeve. It was in pretty good shape considering the use it had. How many miners poured out their woes or shared their joys at this bar rail he wondered?

Mark walked to the staircase which led upstairs when he noticed another door leading to the back of the building. More than likely a storage room he thought to himself. Maybe it's best if I wait for the others before I venture upstairs. The floor could be rotted out and I don't want to take a fall. In the meantime, I can take a look around in the back room instead.

As he turned the doorknob, he could hear rustling and movement inside. "Hmmm, mice," he thought to himself.

The room smelled dank and was pitch black except for a small glimmer of light that fell from the rotted roof. He pointed his flashlight to the ceiling and then to the floor making sure nothing would encumber him when suddenly the light picked up something large standing in the corner!

Perhaps it was the size of the object that made him take two steps back and out of the room. It startled him. Taking a few seconds to compose himself he went back outside, around the back of building and removed the weather-worn boards from the window and door leading to the storage room. It allowed air and light into the sealed room. He had to know what hid in the corner of the room. Before long, the rotten boards gave way to the storage area of the old saloon revealing a treasure that Mark would save from the wrecking ball and a watery grave.

An hour later his crew arrived to begin the destruction of Credence. His foreman found him dusting away filth and cobwebs from a very old piano.

"Wow! It looks like you discovered something pretty special this time," his voice filled with astonishment.

"I'm going to take this home. It's too fine to be

destroyed. It's a mess for sure, but worth restoring," Mark replied in a serious tone.

His foreman nodded in agreement. He knew nothing about antiques, but he recognized the beauty that lay hidden under years of neglect.

"It's been a home to mice and spiders. Not any longer. Get some of the guys to help me move it out of the building. I'll pay them overtime to get it back home," he said.

"Maybe we should save some of the other things too?" the foreman replied.

"I was thinking the same thing. The piano is all I want. We'll leave this building last so everyone can load up what things they like. The whole place is worth salvaging, even the sign. Ask the guys if they want the sign. If not, I'll take that home too. I've seen this before in other condemned buildings. Some of the pieces were just too heavy or the occupants had no use for antiques. Times and tastes change. It's the 20th century and many see this as nothing but a relic and not worth the effort. Well, the owners are long gone just like this place will be soon," Mark said with just a hint of sorrow.

Mark Kinney's profession was engineering, but his passion was history. The old two-story house he shared with his wife, Elizabeth, and three children was packed to the rafters with antiques. His massive collection consisted of books, furniture and art. He found value in anything that told a story. Elizabeth, grateful for his safe return from the war, never scolded him for his ever-growing collection that transformed their home into a time machine. His children found a neverending source of amusement, as well as perfect show and tell assignments. Their imaginations were fueled by his findings.

That evening the venerable, old piano stood in Mark's garage waiting to be restored to its former glory, as well as tell its story. He mentioned to Elizabeth it belonged in the living room, front and center where it could be admired.

"Yes, it will look perfect," she agreed.

After dinner Elizabeth found her husband in the garage, studying something. "What have you got there?" she asked.

"Honey, take a look," he answered quietly.

Mark held out a brittle, yellowed section of sheet music with faded names and notes scribbled on it.

"Seems our old piano held some surprises!" he said with excitement. The music holder folds in and out and can be hidden from view. Look at all this sheet music. Imagine? I wonder who these people were and what kind of lives they led? It really is a wonderful find don't you think?"

"Let me see if I can read their names. My eyesight is better than yours," she laughed.

"Gwenna, Lily Ann, Ginger Fitz, Henry, Denis, there is more writing but it's too faded. Oh, how mysterious. Did you see this?" she added.

"What?" Mark answered.

"Mark, it's a kind of ledger slip, date of delivery, August 15, 1875 signed Cadan Gray. Tomorrow is August 15. What are the chances?" she replied with excitement.

"You can't be serious," he replied.

"I will polish and clean it tomorrow. Maybe I should call a tuner," she added.

"Sounds like you have plans for it already," he said rubbing his eyes and yawning.

"It's full of romance, can't you feel it? It's almost animated. Oh my, I love it already. Well, it's getting late. I better check on the kids. You coming to bed?" she asked.

"Just let me put some things away and turn off the lights," he answered.

Kissing him on the cheek she said, "I'm really happy you brought it home."

He was still excited about his discovery. Nobody on the crew wanted The Nugget sign, so he packed it along. It gave him a sense of peace knowing he and his team saved some of the rich history of the mining settlement. A sensible man, Mark was acutely aware of the benefits of progress. Nevertheless, he knew the past often suffered and fell victim to it. He had a weakness for nostalgia and the piano was more than a piano to him, it was bit of a storyteller. But, unbeknownst to him, it was also a bit of a ghost.

♬ ♪ ♫

Gwenna Steele
Cornwall England, 1849

The morning mist lifted, revealing a glistening spring day as Gwenna passed through the forest on the road to Glencove. Dew sparkled like crystal on meadow grass delighting her with prisms of color. Birds, fresh from their night's slumber, sang cheerfully making her forget her long trek. Nature's peace enfolded her.

The beautiful, small framed girl was filled with hope holding her few belongings, thrilled to be the new parlor maid at the tender age of fourteen. Gwenna would soon be wearing the tidy uniform of the great manor house, Glencove, which would set her apart from her old life. The morning was filled with promise.

Every now and then a passing cart filled with produce or goods would meet her going in the opposite direction. Drivers and passengers would greet her with a smile or hello. Some wondered where the little dark-haired girl with soft brown eyes was headed and why she was alone. But there was something about her demeanor, a sort of calm determination that was uncommon in one so young and they did not question her. Mr. Gray, the Steward of Glencove, noticed it while watching the girl toil for her parents when he stopped by for rents in the village and nearby farms. He respected her neatness and uncomplaining manner. It struck him she was too refined and sweet to be treated harshly by anyone and certainly not by her parents. If anyone deserved a better life, it was Gwenna he thought to himself. He witnessed the ill treatment and brow beating she suffered from her mother who was a discontented, thin lipped woman no doubt jealous of her daughter. For her mother had never been a beauty with a kind disposition. It was a mystery to Silas Gray how anyone so disagreeable could bear such á beauty. It was no wonder her father spent more hours at the local pub than at his downtrodden home. No man, drunk or sober could stomach such a hag. Gwenna no doubt took the brunt of her mother's discontent.

For that reason, Silas Gray felt concern for Gwenna. She always took it upon herself to be a dutiful daughter and mother to her two younger brothers, William and James. She feared her mother's wrath not only for her cruel tongue, but her fists. It was Gwenna who kept the house clean, cooked the meals, did the laundry, and nursed them all when they were ill. She planted the garden and tended the chickens, milked their old cow and all uncomplainingly. She had a sense of duty, a sort of innate responsibility for the whole household. She longed to learn how to embroider but had no time to learn. Her days were spent in drudgery instead. She yearned for a better life but had no way of obtaining it. Still, she set her mind to shouldering responsibilities that were not hers. Gwenna never had a childhood. All the village knew and took pity on the unfortunate girl. For years they watched with sadness as she worked tirelessly while being mistreated. If they tried to intervene, Gwenna paid the price with a bruised lip, or red mark on her cheek. She had become a scapegoat for her ill-tempered mother. It wasn't as if her father was an evil man, but he was a weak one. He had no spine or ambition. Having been injured years ago in the mine, he became a source of shame for the whole family. He would only work a few days a month, complain of his pain, and spend his days begging for drinks. Silas Gray could have evicted them years ago if not for his affection for Gwenna.

As she journeyed on, she glimpsed something crumpled on the side of the narrow road. Getting closer, she noticed a tiny framework of feathers and wings still fluttering in the soft breeze. It was as if the tiny swallow had simply fallen from the sky as there were no signs of a struggle. The joy she felt just minutes ago escaped leaving a kind of emptiness in its wake. Looking around, she found a sliver of bark, lifted the lifeless bird and placed it under a nearby tree. She could not bear the thought of it being trampled by a passing cart, but she also wondered if perhaps the dead songbird was somehow a premonition.

After many hours, Gwenna caught sight of the imposing Elizabethan mansion, Glencove, home of the powerful Eliot family. She forgot her hunger and weariness at the sight of it perched on a hill. Its picturesque beauty was like something out of a fairy tale. Gwenna sheepishly walked slowly through the park-like grounds noticing deer grazing lazily. She was waved on by the gate keeper who no doubt expected her. Early spring blooms and an ornamental pond graced the entrance. She had no idea the vast gardens alone sat on twenty acres, or the estate had its own sawmill, fine stable, and a small 14th century church. The looming mansion held fine art, tapestries, and vast a collection of treasures from all over the world accumulated by generations of the powerful family.

Many people lived and worked at Glencove Manor from the Land Steward, Mr. Gray, all the way to those who held menial jobs. Some of the positions were: head housekeeper, butlers of various rank, cooks or various rank, valet, footmen, nurse, chamber maids, parlor maid, kitchen maids, scullery maid, laundry maid, stable master, grooms, grounds keeper, head gardener and gate keeper. There was no need for a nanny as Richard, the Lord's son was grown. He spent years away at various boarding schools in Europe. Nor was there a need for a ladies maid as his mother was deceased. Still, the house had frequent visitors all year that often stayed for extended periods which required a full staff.

Soon after her arrival, Gwenna met Mrs. Woods, the head housekeeper. Mrs. Woods, although strict, was fair minded. Gwenna listened quietly and attentively to her directions realizing much depended on her following orders and doing each task well.

It was soon evident Gwenna took pride in her new position and worked diligently. Each sitting room and drawing room were exquisitely lovely and pristine after she left them. Day after day, she could be seen darting from one wing to another like an iridescent hummingbird. When her duties were complete and met inspection, she spent time looking at the magnificent grounds. Mrs. Woods appreciated Gwenna's quiet industriousness and dedication. For Glencove never shined so brightly. Therefore, she was granted permission to stroll the endless gardens when time allowed. It was a paradise to her with all manner of plants, flowers, vines, and trees. Thankfully, it was a paradise without a serpent. Over time, her love of flowers caught the attention of the head gardener, George. No one had shown quite the interest and appreciation for the gardens he tended so meticulously before. Since George had never married nor had children, he lavished love on what he held most dear, the magnificent gardens and his little bay filly, Leaf. After working all day in the garden, George would devote the remainder of the evening with his beloved little horse. The Stable Master, Albert, was his brother so Leaf was always well cared for during the day. Leaf had been a weak, sickly foal and not expected to survive. George had witnessed the birth of the little creature and for some inexplicable reason, begged Sir Charles if he could try to save her. George could coax a tiny seed to grow into a mighty vine and he felt confident he could do the same for the tiny foal. Charles felt it was useless, but if by some miracle the foal could be saved, George could certainly have her. Sir Charles Eliot was always a fair-minded individual. He was moved with George's sincerity. Besides, he had a stable full of horses that he enjoyed spending time with.

With Albert's horse expertise and George's constant nurturing, the little filly miraculously grew stronger and began to nurse. At three she was stunningly beautiful, with a gleaming mahogany brown coat, black tips, socks, flowing mane and a tail that swept the ground. Her eyes were large and expressive. Everyone felt Leaf knew it was George who brought her back to life and loved him as horses sometimes do their people. Indeed, she was his greatest treasure and he doted on her.

Just as George nurtured Leaf, so did Gwenna with the noble old house. Her attention to even the tiniest detail created an ambiance unequaled in all of England Vibrant florals complimented each of the vast rooms that she took charge over. Their subtle fragrances floated in the air. It became commonplace for guests to praise Charles on his home and hospitality.

Likewise, the women on the staff often found themselves the recipients of cheerful florals to brighten their mundane lives because of thoughtful Gwenna. Over time, George thought of her as the daughter he never had. She in turn enjoyed his lessons on flowers, trees, fruit and vegetables. She was becoming quite a botanist.

But the eight-foot high yew maze intrigued her the most. The secret garden with its myriad twists and turns was a complicated puzzle. Those who walked through it often found themselves confused. It was situated on one half acre with close to half mile of paths. In the center of the maze stood a life size statue of an angel. It had been placed there by Charles to honor his late wife. It took Albert over six years of constant care to complete the curving, branching maze. One could easily get lost in it for hours if they were not familiar with it. The maze truly was a lesson in trial and error.

George proved to be a fine teacher and friend to Gwenna. He enjoyed sharing his knowledge as she was constantly curious and a quick study. No doubt, Gwenna brought new life to the rooms of the venerable old estate and cheer to all who resided within it. She did not possess a selfish or vengeful heart. Without being asked, she would help anyone if they felt ill or weary never once sparing herself. She was a beacon of light and possessed a spirit so sweet it seemed unreal. Some on the staff felt she was more angel than human. By the end of two years, she was beloved by the household. Naturally, many young men who worked at the estate were drawn to her. Some were quite enamored. Her sweet smile and innocent doe eyes with their unusual gold specks drew them in. Yet, she treated them more like brothers rather than suitors. They soon realized she had no interest in romantic love, at least with them. Like Mr. Gray and George, everyone felt protective of her. For far too long Glencove held a sense of brooding and sorrow that permeated each corner. When she arrived, it felt like spring after an endless dreary winter. The huge old manor was magnificent once again just as it had when the Ladyship lived there years ago.

She was grateful for this opportunity at a new life. Being sensible and mature beyond her years, she was mindful it was a step above housemaid or scullery maid whose daily chores were harsh reminders of how far she had come from the little stone cottage she shared with her parents and brothers. There was often never enough food, so she shared what little she had on her plate with them. Her heart could never refuse. It was just her way to be thoughtful and kind to her co-workers in the same way. In a sense they became her new family. Although she missed her brothers, she was extremely happy her mother could no longer browbeat her. Her quarters were modest, but not to Gwenna when she crawled into the small wooden framed bed with its warm wool blankets, clean white linens and fluffy pillow. Demure in size, the room was bright where sunlight and starlight sparkled through. She slept on a hard cot in the old cottage and had only a thin, worn quilt to keep out the drafts at night. In the winter she slept in her clothing it got so bitterly cold. Here, she had a tiny side table, candles, her own chamber pot, and small wardrobe to hang her uniforms, old dresses, and shawl. She saved her money, only buying a little hand mirror, brush and comb. Her only weakness was the fragrant soaps used at the manor. She was not used to such luxuries and placed a bar on her nightstand so she could breathe in the fragrance. Each night before she fell asleep, she said evening prayers which included not only her family, but mysterious Mr. Gray for rescuing her from her old life of drudgery.

For years Silas Gray observed Gwenna from afar. Sometimes they would see one another in passing and exchange words. It pleased him greatly to see her thrive. For she was not only beautiful on the outside, but her spirit was as well. He respected her for all she had been through and how hard she worked to create a life for herself.

He was ten years older and a bachelor. He never was drawn to another woman as much as her. He felt many were far too vain for no reason, spoiled or lazy. He held a powerful position which drew admiration from both mothers and their daughters hoping to land a rich husband. He was a good judge of character and savvy man of the world who exuded confidence. He trusted few people. He was well educated and had traveled extensively. He was known to be a man of logic and sound judgment.

However, for some inexplicable reason, he found himself constantly thinking of the charming maid. It caught him off guard. Though he concentrated on his many responsibilities, his mind would always wander back to her which made him feel foolish. He was aware of their differences, but he realized she was a cut above the rest no matter where she came from. For honesty and integrity mixed with kindness were rare commodities in Silas Gray's world. Ironically, he had no idea the girl had fallen in love with him long ago, but felt he was far above her station in life.

As time passed, Gwenna heard about Richard Eliot in hushed whispers. The staff all felt a sense of loyalty working for Charles because he was decent and generous to everyone who worked for him not only on his estate, but mines and farms. It confused them to think that such a noble man and beautiful, gentle woman could have conceived such a troubled, dangerous son. Tragically his mother died while giving birth to him, her only child. Therefore, the rearing of him fell upon the widower, Charles and numerous nannies.

From the time he was a young child he brought nothing but pain to anyone or anything who crossed his path. His father could not retain a nanny for the boy because he terrified them with his dangerous temper and strange way. They witnessed his cruel treatment of animals that sickened and frightened them. If they tried to correct his behavior, he lashed out physically often seriously injuring them. One nanny mysteriously tripped down a flight of stairs breaking her leg. Another had a fork stuck in her hand. One unfortunate nanny was punched so hard in her stomach she passed out. Richard even bit the cheek of an unfortunate young nanny leaving an ugly permanent scar. He spat at them, called them foul names, and devised unusual methods to destroy their peace of mind. He had a need to inflict harm and punish from an early age. He was sadistically cruel.

Many unfortunate, innocent animals were left crippled,

blind or broken beyond repair. Animals instinctively knew he was dangerous, could smell evil and bolted. Those that fled undetected were the lucky ones. He used his horses harshly, running some until they dropped. He enjoyed kicking or whipping them if they did not perform as he wished. Many fine and gentle horses were left lame, thus rendered useless and mercifully destroyed. Angered and horrified, Charles would send his horses to a friend or neighbor's stable rather than take a chance on Richard's unpredictable outbursts. Both George and Albert secretly wished one of the horses would seal Richard's fate finally ridding the world of his darkness.

It was the popular consensus that Richard posed a considerable threat. Richard was a human plague. He hunted to kill for sheer pleasure never intending to eat the game. He had a lust for suffering and enjoyed seeing fear in his victims.

The only time the household or nearby villages felt secure were the years Richard was somewhere far away studying or traveling. Everyone hoped he would never return to make their lives miserable.

Somehow, he managed to escape the vengeance of many a man or woman. Hearing of his son's misdeeds and crimes, Charles would pay immense fines, or send victims vast sums in retribution. Richard never once showed remorse for his crimes against anyone nor did he show gratitude towards his father for constantly bailing him out.

He was born without a conscience. He had no moral code, no ethics, no fear of God. He looked upon women and girls as things, not human beings. Those born without a title or wealth were targets and mistreated horribly. He seemed immune from punishment because of his powerful family name and rank.

His fine looks and impeccable clothing belied his depraved nature and many a foolish girl fell prey to his charm. They did not heed warnings of others and recklessly fell into his web of deceit. They were not only victimized but humiliated in a sadistic manner. Nothing interested him more than innocence as he seemed born without it. Nothing thrilled him more than to steal it from others or see life slowly go out in them.

Now, at twenty-two, he was the embodiment of cruelty disguised behind an extremely handsome mask. Standing at over six feet with wavy wheat-blond hair, fine features and crystal blue eyes, he looked more like a prince in a fairy tale than a monster. Still, there was a tangible presence of evil that fine clothing, manners or education could not cloak from those he came into close contact with.

The ominous day came when Charles asked his faithful staff to gather for an announcement. Looking at his grave expression they knew it was a serious matter. Older servants prayed it was not the news they feared most, Richard's return.

Sighing, Charles looked each of them in the eye and said, "Richard, will be here next week after being away for many years."

The room grew silent. There was an uneasiness amongst them. They understood their lives would not be the same. Now, they would be on constant guard, looking behind their backs when walking down long corridors or alone concentrating on their tasks. The monster was returning, and the grand old manor house became morose to match the mood of all those within its walls.

Even though Gwenna was troubled by the stories she heard, she tried to be rational. Perhaps Richard had somehow reformed and his past was filled with exaggeration she thought to herself. She simply could not phantom anyone being so horrible. Her practical side told her to remain consistent with her duties. Furthermore, she had no reason to fear anybody or anything until given just cause. Her intellect told her to calm down, but her intuition told her otherwise.

♬ ♫ ♪

Richard Eliot

The staff were assembled in subdued groups according to position and rank as they pensively awaited Richard's arrival. They stood quietly with an occasional nervous toe tapping now and then. As the fashionable coach could be seen in the distance, Gwenna looked at the faces of her friends. Gone were the smiling jovial ones she grew to love, replaced with vacant expressionless ones. Some of her co-workers seemed to have aged. She knew then, they had not exaggerated the claims of his behavior. Their eyes no longer held a light but appeared dimmed and defeated, their faces pale, mask-like. In truth, she did not realize until that moment how terrified the assemblage was.

She quickly looked up to the azure blue, cloudless day to gain perspective on what was taking place. Surely on such a fine June day nothing dreadful could take place.

The resplendent coach came to a halt. It's magnificent matching black team, were frothy and wild-eyed. Clearly, they had been put through their paces. A footman quickly opened the carriage door for its lone passenger. As Richard stepped out, Gwenna took note of his fashionable, opulent attire. But his cold superior demeanor caused her to take a small step and cower a little. Except for his father and the always unflinching Mr. Gray, he looked at no one as if they did not exist. However, just as the three of them entered the house, someone caught Richard's attention — the small dark-haired doe-eyed girl standing quietly with her group. She did not move or look around to meet his vacant gaze, but still felt a sudden chill that struck fear in her heart.

Days, weeks and months passed without incident. A glimmer of hope began to take root in many of the household. Perhaps a change for the better took place with Richard after all. One could only hope. But the older, wiser members of the household felt it was naïve, premature thinking.

On a brilliant August Sunday afternoon, Gwenna decided to take a walk through the yew maze. It had always been her favorite place to dream, pray and think about Mr. Gray who she missed as he was often away. She never called him Silas, as it was not proper.

She was lost in the moment and failed to notice Richard in the shadows waiting to ambush her. Lurching from behind he spun her around and pushed her backwards into the maze breaking down many of its branches. What started out as a tranquil stroll turned into a nightmare as the green walls closed in upon her.

She let out a scream. He quickly clasped his hand over her mouth, tilted his head back and forth and studied her closely as one does a specimen under a microscope. Smiling he said, "Shhhh little maid, nobody can hear you. Besides, you won't be missed. I haven't decided yet what to do with you. I have an idea, but what do you think I should do with you?" His jeering contorted face was that of a gargoyle and icy crystal blue eyes morphed into a sort of chalky white. She saw nothing but depravity in his serpent eyes.

Earlier, Sir Charles and George were standing in the area discussing plans for a greenhouse when they spotted Gwenna enter the maze. It troubled them. They realized Richard was somewhere on the grounds and he was never to be trusted. George excused himself and took chase through the maze shouting, "Gwenna, where are you?" Charles trailed behind fearful of what could be taking place.

Hearing George shout, Richard backed away from the shaken girl. George and Charles met him as he casually passed them on the path. Smiling he greeted his father and shot George a look so filled with hatred that it frightened both men. George had vexed his plans and would pay.

Broken branches and debris were strewn everywhere as if a hurricane had ripped through. The sight of trembling Gwenna clutching her blouse shocked them more. She was silent, but her terrified eyes told them something dreadful happened. She was safe from harm, but for how long?

A week after the incident, Charles and Mr. Gray told the staff they were leaving for two weeks and taking Richard with them. They left quietly early one day with no fanfare. Gwenna had said nothing about the terrifying encounter with Richard and wished to keep it a secret. She simply told Mrs. Woods she felt ill and needed to rest. It was unusual because she never took time for herself and everyone grew concerned. They did not pry but had an inkling who was responsible. George and Silas felt she needed to be guarded. While some of the staff wondered if Richard was being placed in a hospital for observation others felt he belonged in prison.

With Richard absent, the household could feel somewhat secure. However, a few of them questioned whether it was worth working and living at Glencove if such a dangerous person was back in their midst. The mines, although dangerous, at least did not have a monster lurking. It would not be an easy decision. Many held hope he would leave for years on end as he did before. Most wished him dead.

One morning a letter came for Gwenna stating her mother had fallen gravely ill and was not expected to live. She was needed at home and must leave immediately. It was a troubling letter and she brought it to Mrs. Woods asking her advice. Mrs. Woods felt it best for her not to go. Nevertheless, if she insisted at least travel with a chaperone. For it was not wise for a young woman to travel alone. Nevertheless, she had traveled by herself two years ago without incident. Somehow the letter seemed contrived to Mrs. Woods and she was uneasy. Who would have written a letter on such fine stationary, certainly no one from Gwenna's poverty stricken family. "Perhaps the vicar at the church wrote it," Gwenna said quietly. Yet, it mattered not who wrote the letter because she had already started to pack her little bag. She was needed at home to care for them. "Don't worry, I'll return once I'm no longer needed." meaning when her mother had passed.

♫ ♪ ♫

Dark Forest

Gwenna walked briskly only taking brief moments to catch her breath. The late September morning grew warm and with no breeze. It was important to arrive in the village before nightfall. It wasn't wise for anyone to travel alone at night. Every now and then a cart would meet her along the path as before. As before, they would greet her with a nod or wave as they passed, otherwise, she was alone on the road back to the village

By early afternoon she was extremely hungry. Lovingly, the cook prepared a little feast for her journey. Gwenna tucked a napkin under her chin and bodice being mindful of not staining her uniform she wore with such pride. Since Glencove staff were given three sets of uniforms she was able to wear one. Her bag contained two clean but worn dresses, a brush, comb, under garments and simple toiletries. Once in the humble cottage, she would slip into one of the old dresses and shoes. But, she wanted to enter the village in her dignified uniform for all to see.

She savored every bite of roast beef tucked between bread, a tart apple, and generous piece of sponge cake. The lunch refreshed her and gave a needed boost of energy.

Once done eating, she picked up her pace. She pulled out the dainty canteen filled with cool water the cook loaned her. She took a long sip and studied the refined little water vessel. It was lovely. Gwenna assured the cook she would return the container when she returned sensing it must have held special meaning. In fact, it had been a christening gift to the cook on the birth of her baby from the Ladyship long ago. It was one of the cook's greatest treasures. Her daughter having died young of an undetermined cause remained a mystery decades later. However, many people had their thoughts and theories on what could have possibly happened to an otherwise happy healthy child to suddenly die while playing.

The cook, along with the others, worried for Gwenna's safety. No one knew how long she would be gone to care for her ailing mother and family. They begged her to wait for someone on the staff to accompany her. Gwenna assured them if she could walk to Glencove alone without escort two years ago, she could do it again. She had to make haste. As usual, she was not concerned with her welfare but that of others.

Paying little heed to her sore feet and legs, she continued, cheered at the thought of seeing her little brothers who were not far. Oh, how tall they must be by now she thought. The village was a half hour away, just beyond the woodland. The sun was lowering in the sky. Soon it would be dusk. She felt a cool welcoming breeze brush her face and body. But, before long, the welcoming breeze turned decidedly cold, almost menacing. Feeling a slight chill, she wrapped her soft shawl around her shoulders. Gwenna looked up and noticed a flock of birds fly from the woodland ahead scatter in all directions. It was a strange sight and she wondered what had unsettled them from their refuge. Getting closer to the forest, she reflected on what she might encounter in the stone cottage she once considered home. Though her mother always mistreated her, Gwenna felt a sense of duty towards her. She also realized her father would need her more than ever to cook, clean and help them if her mother died. Even though they were still boys, they worked in the mines which greatly troubled her. Her father was unable to provide not only because of his alcoholism, but the severity of his old injuries from decades spent in brutal conditions. That was the reason she sacrificed half her month's wages to them.

Within a few minutes she came to the edge of the forest where two paths intersected. One path led through the forest into her family's village. The other skirted the forest to neighboring villages and beyond. Entering the woodland, she noticed gnarled trees, some splayed out in all directions. One looked like an earth octopus and it made her uneasy to look upon it. Many seemed to have menacing faces etched in their bark and she felt as though they were watching as she walked swiftly by. She scolded herself for her foolish thoughts. Still, never had she felt such gloom and she picked up her pace, even more focused on what she would encounter once inside her parent's cottage. She would not allow her imagination to run wild. The ancient woodland had an unnatural silence and no signs of wildlife which struck her as odd. She recalled seeing deer, fox, rabbits and songbirds when she traveled along its path two years ago in spring. It was a cacophony of happy sounds, soft shades of green and sweet fragrances. Now, it was lifeless, dank and musty. Likewise, the ancient trees were not arrayed in brilliant fall colors but dressed in faded brown, drab yellow and moldy black, adding to the dreariness.

Many of the centuries old hawthorns were contorted in unusual shapes by the wind. Massive oaks dominated the ancient forest. Some were so large one could easily live in them. Moss and lichen hung down and covered most of the trees adding to the mood. Trees like ash, elm, juniper and dogwood made up the dense forest making it nearly impossible to see beyond the path. She was small, yet the path seemed to narrow in places making it difficult to navigate. Strange, she did not recall the path posing such problems before. But it had been spring. Trees, shrubs and vines were just beginning to emerge she told herself. Likewise, some of the branches reached down, touching her head and shoulders, snatching her blouse making her feel like a rabbit in a snare. One held a large web whose strands clung to her sleeve containing a bulbous black spider which terrified and revolted her. Frantically brushing it off, she was relieved to see it creep into the undergrowth. She checked her hair and clothing to make certain there were no webs. Finding none, she continued at a trot.

It was hard to envision this was the same forest that held colorful carpets of blue bells, wood anemone, yellow archangel and primrose in spring. It delighted and cheered travelers through the ages. But, in fall and winter the ancient forest became a place of mystery and legend. She tried to push down tales of it being haunted while walking under the looming branches that shrouded the sun. Nature could be arbitrary, sometimes gentle, sometimes dangerous and cruel, like people. Only a few streaks of light penetrated the narrow walkway. She became more anxious and regretted not taking the sound advice of Mrs. Woods on traveling alone.

In the distance she saw someone standing on the path holding the reins of a tall horse. Her heart stopped, then began racing. She was unable to discern the figure in the shadows. It was too late for her to hide as the figure already spotted her. The entrance was some distance back and the unknown rider was standing at the exit which continued to the village. She realized she had no choice but continue. Just then, the figure mounted the horse and headed in her direction. She stood transfixed before she scrambled off the path and began running, stumbling over tree stumps and fallen branches. The sound of cracking tree limbs was not far behind. Though she was exhausted from her long walk, she managed to muster strength to run, not heeding the lashes of branches and thorny shrubs on her face and arms. Her right shoe fell off as she ran and her once pristine uniform ripped to pieces. Her body was bathed in sweat and her heart felt as if it would burst. She turned her head from side to side frantically searching for a place to hide but it was hopeless. Gwenna was no match for the horse and rider. Crashing through the forest, the horse and rider would soon be upon her. Her limbs were wobbly and weak. Spent, she fell backwards onto the forest floor. Before she could regain her footing, the horse's hooves were within inches of her. She thought she would be stomped to death. It was then she noticed blood running down the horse's trembling legs and side from being spurred and scrapping against the thorn branches. She knew without looking up who the rider was!

Gwenna had been trapped in the forest for two hours but it felt like an eternity. Large oak branches hovered above her, bearing witness of her brutal assault. Only after Richard rode away did she dare crawl from the sullied evil place. She was like a panic-stricken rabbit throughout her ordeal, silent except for a muffled cry. In shock, she had no idea the severity of her injuries. She was covered in welts and scratches. Some were sustained as she ran through the forest, others at Richard's hands. Her insides burned and ached. Her face, lips and mouth were swollen and red. Her head ached and was spinning. She noticed blood on her legs, arms and clothing and realized it was hers. Under her broken fingernails she noticed dried blood, the results of clawing his face which only served to goad him on. Soon she would be covered with ugly bruises. Strands of her beautiful dark brown hair had been ripped when he pulled her down by her head to the hard ground. Her clothing was in shreds and laid to waste just as she had been. She looked at the place where her innocence had been spilled. Her pain and terror turned to shame. She knew if anyone found out what happened she would be blamed and considered ruined so powerful was Richard's family name. I am ruined she thought and felt it would have been a blessing if God could take her life at that moment. She was filled with despair and wept.

Some minutes passed before she slowly crawled on the damp forest floor in search of her bag and shawl. The silver canteen was missing. She felt parched and feverish. She desperately needed a sip of water. She remembered the small stream that ran next to the forest. Fearing Richard would return, she hastily pulled on one of her old dresses. Extremely weak, she managed to crawl only a short distance. Finally, she willed herself up with the help of a low tree limb. She steadied herself and took a small step, then another. She worked her way towards the exit all the while fearing Richard might return to murder her.

Her mind and body were reeling. She had to think of an excuse to explain the injuries. No one could find out what took place. Gwenna realized she could never return to Glencove or her friends. She felt a stabbing pain once again inside her. She was severely battered and desperately needed help, but there was no one. The physical and emotional torture she endured would forever be embedded in her soul.

As she whispered a childhood prayer, a streak of sunlight slipped through the dense canopy and on her beautiful tear-stained face. She gathered her brokenness and crept away like a broken animal. Hiding in tall grasses until nightfall, weak from hunger, dirty and bloodied, she prayed again for courage and strength. At last she found herself at the banks of the babbling little stream undetected. She looked around and listened. It was silent except for an owl hooting in the distance.

It was twilight. Her hand was shaking while she cupped the clean cool water to her broken lips. It helped clear her head and she remembered a scented soap and soft towel set she planned on giving her mother tucked away in her bag. Using them, she washed her face, and body in the cold water, careful not to hurt herself more. Gwenna tried to fix her hair knowing what a mess it had to be, some of it in knots, covered with dirt. She slowly combed it. But it became too painful where strands had been torn out. Her little head hung in sorrow as her beautiful eyes filled once more with tears.

As darkness covered the small village, she knocked on the rough-hewn door. To her shock her mother answered saying, "What are you doing here? You look a fright. So, they threw you out of the fine manor house. Well, don't expect us to feed you girl. You better go find work in the mines with your brothers if you expect to live under my roof."

Gwenna's mother had never been on her death bed after all. It was simply a cruel hoax, handiwork of Richard.

♫ ♫ ♫

Goodbye

Gwenna never told a soul what happened to her. She said nothing other than the Head Housekeeper let her go and she simply fell down while walking. Her mother seemed to back down after seeing her daughter's injuries and for once, held her tongue. Her father looked bewildered and broken hearted after noticing the bruises and marks on his daughter. He loved her in his own way. It frightened and confused him to see her so broken. Her brothers were thrilled to have her once again in their midst, but they too felt something had changed in their sweet sister. Even though she felt ill, and needed time to heal, she somehow managed to help her mother as before. Likewise, she assured her parents she would be searching elsewhere for employment which was true. In the meantime, she ate little and remained unnaturally quiet. She only stepped outside the cottage to empty buckets or hang wash. Old neighbors were surprised to see pretty Gwenna back home and soon began whispering.

While her parents and brothers slept, she lay awake reliving the nightmare that took place in the forest. She feared she was with child more than anything. What would become of me, or my child she thought to herself.

On the fourth week of her return she woke before dawn feeling sick. She managed to get outside so nobody could hear her. She hoped it was something she ate, but none of the others were ill. When she continued to feel sick each morning and sometimes during the day it became a concern. She no longer could hide her queasiness. Her hard faced mother looked at her daughter's beautiful, pale face one morning and bluntly stated "I know you got yourself with child. You have disgraced us. You are no longer welcome here. Besides, we don't have money to feed you or your bastard. Do you even know who the father is? I thought I raised you better than that. No wonder they let you go."

Packing what little she had, Gwenna once more set out, only this time still healing from her attack and sick with child. Her father was disconsolate to see her leave and pleaded with her to stay. But living with her bitter mother was useless. She had suffered too much brutality to endure more. She had no choice but to leave and not look back. Her father turned and went into the tiny room he shared with his wicked wife. He came back carrying his only family heirloom, a small brass and mahogany monocular spyglass. It would fit into her little bag easily. When extended it was 12 inches with a circumference of 2 inches. Fully extended it was 24 inches. One of his uncles served in the British Navy and her father inherited the instrument. As Gwenna walked out the door, he caught her in his arms and placed it in her hands. Choking he said, "Look forward sweet Gwenna, never look back!" She looked into his watery, world worn eyes and realized it was all he had to give her. Never had she loved him more and forgave him for being such a poor excuse of a father. For they both knew it was the last time either one of them would see each other in life. Outraged and jealous, her mother started to berate the girl once again. Her father turned around and looked at his wife with such a look of hatred it frightened her. She knew she had crossed the line and did not utter another word.

Her brothers followed her, James carrying her little bag. Nosy neighbors stood in their doorways desperately trying to hear what was being said. William and James begged her to stay. However, she knew it would be only bringing gossip and disgrace to them.

James, the younger brother, started to cry. Gwenna stopped and gently took her bag from him. She embraced him saying, "There is no need to worry. We will see each other again one day. I promise."

William, stoically responded, "Yes, we will find you." He hugged her tightly saying, "I am proud of you sister." William had no idea how much his encouraging words meant at that moment.

James chimed in, "You're the finest person I know. Never forget I love you sister."

"You boys don't want to be late for work, It's getting late and I must be on my way," she replied. Both of her brothers were much taller than her, but they appeared like children to Gwenna. "Now, be off and take care of yourselves. Everything will turn out, wait and see," she said in a stern voice trying to make the parting easier on all of them.

Every so often she turned to watch her two strapping brothers in the distance. A feeling of sadness and longing overtook her. With no witnesses, she could finally say prayers aloud for God to protect her and her unborn child from the unknown.

Within an hour she began to falter. The sky was turning gray and mist was covering the land which added to her misery. She needed to stop. Even though her bag was not heavy, she suffered broken fingers on both hands from the attack, making it difficult to hold. In the distance hoof beats could be heard. Not being able to see through the dense fog, she prayed once again.

Within seconds, an ornately painted wagon pulled by a beautiful sweet-faced piebald Cob emerged from the fog. They stopped within a few yards of her. They were a handsome middle age couple dressed in flamboyant, colorful clothing. Seeing her plight, the woman asked, "Miss, would you like to travel with us? We are headed to Looe. We have more than enough to eat if you don't mind sharing the back with Patch. Gwenna recognized them as Romani folk or Gypsies. They were known to tell fortunes and frightened her somewhat. Yet, she was immediately taken with the beautiful and intricate embroidery on their clothing and the woman's jewelry.

"My name is Esmerelda and this is my husband, Andrei. What's your name Miss? "asked Esmerelda, her voice filled with concern.

"I'm Gwenna," was all she had strength to say.

Andrei climbed down to help her into the back of their wagon saying, "You will be alright now Miss Gwenna. Patch will stand guard."

Looking around the comfortable and elaborately decorated wagon she pondered her fate. She was too weary to weep any longer. Patch, sensing her grief, placed his soft head in her lap, begging her to pet him.

"Oh Patch, are you a stray too? Well then, we better stick together," she said gently. Closing her eyes, she whispered, "Please Dear God, I need your help," then closed her eyes and fell fast asleep.

Mild the mist upon the hill
Telling not of storms tomorrow;
No, the day has wept its fill,
Spent its store of silent sorrow.

O, I'm gone back to the days of youth,
I am a child once more,
And 'neath my father's sheltering roof
And near the old hall door .

—Emily Bronte

♬ ♪ ♫

Leaf

As days passed with no word from Gwenna, people became concerned, but none more than Silas Gray. It was not like her to be inconsiderate, especially with her friends and co-workers. Someone would have heard something before now. Surely something was wrong.

Cleaning Richard's room one day, two servants noticed the beautiful silver canteen the cook gave Gwenna. It was Richard's perverse notion of a souvenir sitting on his dressing table. They were fearful of his wrath should he find out they discovered it. So, one servant fetched Mrs. Woods, while the other continued working as if nothing was out of place should he return.

Mrs. Wood's worst fears for Gwenna were confirmed after seeing the canteen. Sir Charles had to be told. Alone in his study, she showed him the evidence. His face turned to stone. He offered her something to drink which she politely declined. However, he filled a large goblet with brandy, drank it all, refilled it and sat down. He seemed to age before her eyes. Looking out the window he said in a low voice, "Get Silas. He'll find her and bring her back. I will deal with Richard."

Charles had hoped the doctors in London cured Richard of the darkness that consumed him. They were reputable physicians, skilled in the medical arts, but they were no match for the cunning and evil of Richard. He simply told them what they wanted to hear and before long he was cured of whatever mental malady or trouble he had. So, he was once more allowed to do whatever he pleased.

Richard was not seen for a few days, so everyone felt he must be in London enjoying some type of depraved entertainment. Instead, he was lurking about the stables in the early hours undetected. He vowed revenge on George for humiliating him in the maze and would stop at nothing to achieve it.

A few days later Leaf was missing. Albert found her stall empty and her hay untouched from the night before. George, Albert and the stable hands searched frantically for her. She was nowhere to be found. Later that afternoon two miners were seen in front of the manor, talking to Sir Charles. Earlier that morning they came across the body of a beautiful, little mahogany brown filly at the bottom of the mine shaft. The miners used a pulley to bring her shattered body to the surface. The usual tough and hardened men were in tears with such a brutal scene. After receiving the news, both George and Albert took chase hoping it wasn't Leaf. But it was.

Seeing her lifeless body, George fell on his knees, took her lovely head in his arms and wept. He kept stroking Leaf's beautiful face, smoothing her mane and petting her lovely coat, now spattered in blood. Her eyes were open, now longer alert and warm, but lifeless and black. Tenderly he shut them. Everyone knew it was no accident as her luxuriant tail had been cut in half. Obviously another souvenir. But nothing frightened Albert more than to see George in such a state. It would take a long time, if ever, for him to be himself again.

When Charles arrived on the scene, the onlookers stood back, out of respect. By now George was inconsolable. As Charles walked by the group of men gathered, a few of them heard Charles mutter "It would have been better that he had never been born. Forgive me, Lord, for bringing such an evil child into this world."

Leaf was loaded onto a wagon and taken home. She was buried under a fine old oak in the pasture adjacent to the stable. She would be near her pasture mates, and close to those who loved her best, George and Albert.

♫ ♫ ♫

Banshee

As Silas Gray searched for Gwenna, Richard managed to remain hidden. Everyone was acutely aware of the danger he posed and remained alert. The authorities were notified regarding the missing parlor maid and Richard Eliot. No longer was Charles willing to protect his son. Weighed down by guilt, he wanted justice for the victims. It was one thing to protect a family member, especially a son or daughter. But it was quite another to allow them safe sanctuary after committing heinous crimes.

A close friend stopped by Glencove to check on Charles. He insisted they attend a local horse auction in a nearby village. "It will do you good to let go of this mess with Richard, if only for a few hours. He will be found. It's only a matter of time. Besides, I need your advice before I make a bid," he said smiling. His friend was concerned knowing Charles had become a sort of recluse, both out of sorrow and shame.

Charles was hesitant at first, he had no interest in buying another horse. The hideous death of Leaf lingered in his thoughts. Yet, something inside told him his friend was right. He needed to clear his head.

Many people came from all around to browse and gossip. Some were gentry, others local farmers and villagers. Seeing Sir Charles, some in the crowd, tipped their hats and greeted him in a cordial manner befitting his station. Yet, others that he knew for years ignored him which cut him to the marrow. Richard's deeds were well known and documented. Furthermore, Charles was often blamed for the sins of his son. Charles felt they had every right to feel so and it pained him greatly. Prior to the sordid notoriety brought about by his Richard, Charles had been well thought of. He had always been considered a man of integrity.

His friend noticed the aloof glances of some and told Charles, "This will pass once Richard is found and brought to justice. Believe me. Things will turn around. Remember, you are here to help me bid on a horse. Ignore them."

As hours passed, the two men spent considerable time studying various horses. Many were splendid and no doubt would fetch quite a sum. There were various breeds and sizes from massive, docile drafts to elegant carriage horses. Sellers held lead ropes while buyers walked around inspecting them. The auction ring became lively. For a brief while it helped Charles forget the looming problems he faced with the missing girl and his dangerous son. True to his word, Charles helped his friend to find two matching dapple- gray geldings. Before they got back to their carriage, they had to walk by a few makeshift stalls. Horses considered unruly or dangerous were held in them for the safety of onlookers. It was in one such stall that Charles stopped to admire a tall, solid black thoroughbred mare. She was stunning. One could see she had fine breeding. She acknowledged him with a soft nicker causing the seller to gasp and say, "Banshee must like you. She has not responded like that before. My wife and I raised her and never once heard her utter a kind sound. Odd indeed! I tell you sir, for all her beauty she is not pleasant. We hoped she would make a fine riding horse or at least a loving brood mare but she refused to be either. We could not work with her and others gave up fearful of her tricks. She strikes fear in everyone that comes too near. I must be honest with you sir. I need to sell her, but beware of her clever ways." Sir Charles appreciated what the man had to say. But by that time Banshee was nuzzling Charles hand, beseeching him to take her home. Charles had to have her despite both the warning of the seller and his friend. When Banshee was led in the ring the crowd was awed by her fine breeding and beauty. However, her behavior was so wild and out of control nobody wanted her except Charles. The crowd went silent as the horse once more came up willingly and docile to him. He paid the seller and had the mare delivered to Glencove.

After Albert heard about the dangerous mare, it baffled him why Charles bought her. It was perplexing to everyone. However, it wasn't his place to question such decisions. His position was to take care and train her. Albert expected the worse. Yet, the next day he was pleasantly surprised to see not only a stunning mare, but a mild mannered one arrive.

Banshee proved to be highly intelligent and gentle. She indicated no signs of her former behavior. It was as if she had already been trained because both Albert and Charles rode her without problems. She seemed to float rather than canter. Never did she kick the stable hands, nor did she act belligerently with other horses. Each day she would gaze in the direction of the gardens where George worked. He purposely avoided the stable area, as it broke his heart not seeing his beloved Leaf grazing or playing in the pasture. He would visit her resting place in early morning and leave a carrot while the other horses were still in their stalls. His little ritual became a daily habit. One morning while he stood alone by her grave, he heard a soft nicker. It was Banshee! It surprised him not knowing what to expect as they stood looking at one another. After a short pause, he reached down and picked up the carrot he left for Leaf and offered it to Banshee. She walked slowly to him with her head down in a submissive manner and accepted the carrot. After she finished, she placed her velvet muzzle next to his hand and breathed deeply. George stroked her splendid neck and mane. "How did you get out girl? We better get you back before the others notice. We don't want you in trouble," he spoke gently. He walked back to the stable to get a lead rope but there was no need as she followed close behind. It was unclear how she escaped as he examined the latch on the stall and found nothing. It remained their secret.

Albert and Charles noticed the unusual behavior of Banshee with George. Whenever she saw him, she would break free of her pasture mates, call out and run to his side. It was obvious, she had chosen George to be her person.

As a month passed, the authorities were still unable to locate Richard, who was now deemed quite mad. Had he left the area or was he hiding under their noses? It was unsettling for everyone.

Days were growing shorter, nights colder and soon it would be winter. It was the last week of November. Just after dawn, on his way to Leaf's resting place, George wondered about celebrating Christmas given the last troubled three months. "How could anyone feel festive?" he thought. Frost had coated everything in its path during the night and it looked pristine. The effect was spectacular. As George trudged along, his boots made a crunching sound on the frozen ground. Otherwise it was silent.

As he drew closer to Leaf's grave which sat on a tiny knoll, he gazed into the meadow below. He would often see deer grazing. It was always a peaceful sight. However, something was different this time. George noticed something dark lying on the ground that didn't move. Curious, he walked down the slope to the frozen meadow to see what the object possibly could be. The landscape fell silent as George approached.

As he drew nearer, he saw a man lying on his back in a large circle surrounded by numerous hoof prints. Observers perhaps? The coating of frost near the man was undisturbed except for one set of hooves. It was a strange scene. The man held his arms protectively around his smashed head. It was obvious, one horse killed him with its hooves as others stood by. George knew better than to disturb the body. He turned and quickly headed back to the stable.

Albert and the stable hands were already up, feeding and grooming horses or cleaning stalls. Not one horse was missing. George noticed Banshee contentedly eating her hay. She nickered a greeting when he walked by, her dark eyes soft with love. He stopped and gently petted her forehead saying, "Good morning, beauty." Albert noticed and smiled. He could see the bond between George and Banshee and it gladdened him. Although no horse could replace Leaf, his love grew each day for the mysterious black mare. No one could possibly phantom how cunning the mare was. But George felt relief knowing she was in her stall that morning along with the others. For he feared she might be blamed for the attack on the man lying in the meadow, Richard.

Charles was visibly shaken at the sight of his wicked son lying in the bizarre circle. He did not need to look at the shattered face to recognize him. His fine clothing and wheat-blond hair covered in blood were enough. For he was after all, his only child and so he wept. Then Charles walked slowly to Richard's body, reached down and touched him lightly.

The authorities were baffled at the strange scene and had little to say. They simply called it a bizarre accident and simply closed the case. It was easier that way for everyone.

♫ ♪ ♫

Dakota Territory, 1875

It was June. Cadan gazed in wonderment at the tall prairie grass. Some of it looked shoulder high or higher, a tenuous sea of undulating waves. It went on forever and it made him feel lonely. Nothing prepared him for such a gigantic landscape of land and sky. Not even Neptune's wrath crossing the Atlantic made him feel less significant than Dakota Territory.

He watched as threatening storm clouds rolled and clashed into one another, turning the azure sky black. They resembled a battalion of war ships. A loud rumble of thunder startled him. Brilliant flashes of lightening zigzagged across the late afternoon sky. He was startled as the scene unfolded and questioned if he had made the right decision on coming here alone. No doubt, the land posed danger. Suddenly, he heard his mother's words, *"Cadan, do not fear thunder. It will not harm you. Remember, it is a warning of the storms you will face later, so ready yourself."*

Dakota Territory was a world away from his orderly home in England. There was no semblance of order here, no pastoral scenes of docile sheep grazing in peaceful, green meadows with stone walls to keep them from wandering into neighboring fields. Nor were there quiet cottages with well -tended flower gardens dotting the landscape. No, this land was untamed and unpredictable. He was shocked to see broken down wagons, goods and furniture left behind and skeletons of animals too weak to continue. But he never could get used to seeing the makeshift graves of pioneers disrupted by scavenging animals. It was a brutal, heartbreaking reality for mourning families to abandon their loved ones in a strange land far from home.

The land teemed with wildlife such as wolves, coyotes, white tail deer, massive bears, cougars, and elk Rather than cattle or sheep grazing lazily, he saw large herds of bison roaming freely on the green-brown prairie. Their thick shaggy coats, massive skulls and rounded hump made them look cumbersome. Yet they were agile and could run fast. It was best not to provoke the huge brown beasts.

The oxen train halted to let the storm pass. The thunder crashed again, followed by a flash of lightening and rain poured from the heavy clouds.

He took out the spy glass his mother gave him before he sailed to America. He peered through it and saw the storm clearing in the horizon. He touched it tenderly, smiled and remembered more of her words, *"Look forward, don't look back."* They were the same words her father told her while placing it in her arms many years ago. He looked up at the immense sky and recalled his mother's wisdom about nature, *"Listen to it, respect it, for nature is another word for God."*

At twenty-three, Cadan Gray wanted to explore the world. His mother, Gwenna, chose the name, Cadan, because it meant battle in old Welsh/Cornish. She felt he could draw strength from it when he faced life's heartbreaks and disappointments. The name suited him well.

He wanted to resolve issues he was faced with and distance would provide it. His spirit bore no resemblance to Richard; yet, it shamed and troubled him to be the offspring of such a despicable man. Although he was never told about the violent union which resulted in his birth, the truth surfaced now and then whether by thoughtlessness, cruelty, or innuendo. It was a heavy burden for him to carry at times and more than likely was the cause of his stuttering. At times it was difficult for him to express himself, so he sought refuge in nature and music.

He had his mother's wonderful, warm brown eyes and infectious smile. Although not tall like Richard, he was tan, robust and muscular from spending time outdoors. Still, his wheat blond hair no doubt came from Richard. Whenever he questioned his mother about his biological father she replied, "You are loved far more than you will ever know and that's what's most important." It was true. Silas Gray was the only father he knew and loved. Silas married Gwenna before he was born and seven when he found out he was adopted. Silas was an amazing husband and father. Yet, as a child he wondered why Sir Charles took such an interest in him. Eventually, when he was old enough to understand, Gwenna told him who his birth father was. She chose her words wisely, not wanting the boy to feel shock or shame. Richard's sins were not his after all. "No child should be less in God's eyes because of his father or mother," Gwenna told him. Silas said much the same, "Remember, we are not to be held accountable for the misdeeds of others. It is their choosing." As profound as the words were, a seed of insecurity grew in the boy.

As time passed, Cadan grew into a tender hearted, inquisitive, bright and respectful boy. Like his mother, Gwenna, he brought joy rather than sorrow. He had a sense of adventure and solid direction. He was unpretentious, unselfish and unassuming. He bore none of his biological father's narcissistic, sadistic nature. He proved a child can be nothing like the parent nor the parent like the child which was a blessing for everyone.

He learned how to work hard by observing his mother in her gardens and household. She never felt a need for a maid even though Silas easily could have provided it. One could say Cadan was a mix of common man and aristocratic refinement. His powerful grandfather made it possible for him to be educated in the finest schools where he proved to be a good student. However, his passion was music, specifically the piano and he had a gift for it. He was by all accounts a child prodigy whose talent delighted and amazed everyone. He not only could play the classics with great depth and feeling, he began composing his own pieces.

Many who heard them were moved to tears. To his mother's delight, he enjoyed playing lively folk music that reminded her of the Romani people who took her in when she was so alone in the world. As if by magic, a piano would come alive whenever Cadan's fingers caressed the keys. His fingers and hands were strong and beautiful. He understood music as only one truly gifted can. If a piece demanded joy it brought smiles, if it demanded sorrow it brought tears, if it demanded anger it brought fury.

The piano expressed in music what Cadan often failed to do in words. Therefore, he was thrilled his grandfather was sending a piano from England once he was settled in the small mining community of Credence. Without a piano he would not be whole.

The oxen train consisted of a diverse group of individuals seeking their fortune in the Black Hills. It could be a perilous, uncomfortable journey. But lust for the gold kept them coming despite unknown dangers. It took fifteen days by oxen train to travel 200 miles from Ft. Pierre to Deadwood through dusty rough terrain, deep gumbo mud, violent storms and hostile Indian territory. Whites were not supposed to enter the Black Hills according to the treaty, but hordes of prospectors, miners, shop keepers, bankers, prostitutes, gamblers, saloon keepers, reckless drifters and foolish dreamers all were headed west. The train was also loaded with much needed supplies for the burgeoning mining communities as well.

In the meantime, the train stalled in the strangely beautiful desolate area known as the Badlands. The towering pinnacles reminded him of castles in Europe but instead were carved from the passage of time. It was a land of canyons, saw-tooth divides, gullies and buttes of delicately banded colors of white, orange, rust, tan, gray, pink and purple. At sunrise and sunset, they were breathtaking. The rugged, ancient geologic wilderness he found himself in was a land of extremes. The Lakota people called it *Mako Sica* or Badland. It was inhospitable with little water which ironically had been an underwater world with the fossils of animals that once roamed millions of years ago.

He was relieved the storm passed, allowing the train to continue its journey. He was anxious to arrive in the settlement named, Credence which was twelve miles from Deadwood.

Part II

As the days passed, Cadan became acquainted with some of the other passengers. Many were seeking adventure and wealth after hearing of the rich gold strike. Cadan had initiative and courage. He was not afraid of hard work, much like his mother. He wanted to test himself and Dakota Territory was just the place. A few miners, as well as a former Civil War doctor, decided to settle in Credence. His name was Dr. Jacob McIntosh. About forty-five, he was a competent, calm and refined individual compared to many of the so-called doctors out west. He reminded Cadan a little of his stepfather, Silas. They both carried themselves well and had thoughtful expressions.

The other passengers comprised of whiskey peddlers, lawyers, land speculators, miners, gamblers, prostitutes, Chinese laborers, shop keepers, lumber men, bankers, even one European opera singer and her entourage were destined for the gold rich mining camp of Deadwood. The opera singer had been hired at an enormous fee to entertain the miners in a newly built hotel-saloon. She remained aloof throughout the whole journey from the other passengers obviously second guessing her decision.

Cadan spotted the outline of the mysterious hills shrouded by clouds and recalled warnings of Sioux unrest caused by broken treaties and more government betrayal. It was wise to be on guard. The hills were rich beyond belief with veins of gold, but they were also filled with extreme danger.

When the oxen train entered the Black Hills, he was taken aback by their beauty. Again, he was amazed with the scenery of Dakota. How varied it was from the endless grassland prairie to the rugged hills filled with pine scent that hung in the air. The passengers journeyed into areas filled with birch, aspen and spruce. Along the creeks, willow trees grew abundantly. Hawks and eagles soared in the sky, the forest was filled with wildlife and the streams with fish. The rocky ground in many places glittered with mica. It looked magical and magnificent. However, it was extremely treacherous because of the sheer altitude. Higher and higher they climbed with their freight wagons. When they reached the summit, they stopped the train. The view was spectacular. The small settlement of Credence sat at the bottom of a gigantic meadow rimmed with trees with a creek running through it.

Slowly they descended into the valley, reaching the mining settlement. A meadowlark sang heartily as if welcoming them. It was early morning and most of the inhabitants were busy working their claims while others were with chores. Shanties, tents, simple wooden structures, framed houses and small hand-hewn log cabins dotted both sides of the street and along hilly ridges. Signs and shutters hung advertising businesses such as Livery Stable, Rosie's Restaurant, Nugget Saloon & Hotel, Credence Bank, Assay Office, Post Office, Eriksson's Hotel & Diner, Dentist, Lumber and two laundries. Sounds of saws and hammers could be heard as Credence was growing rapidly. The lumbering oxen train stopped directly in front of a two story, whitewashed structure with a large, elaborately painted green sign which read: Wolf's Dry Goods. Standing on the steps was no doubt the proprietor, Franz Wolf. He was a prosperous looking man about forty, with thick curly light brown hair, a trimmed handlebar mustache, and round spectacles.

Cadan and Dr. McIntosh climbed down from their wagons, stretched their legs on the dusty street and looked around. The train would only be in the settlement long enough to unload merchandise as they had another twelve miles yet to travel. Cadan and Jacob would call the small mining settlement home for at least a year, if not more. Dr. McIntosh left a prestigious medical practice in Boston much to his wife's dismay. Rather than accompany him out west, she stayed back east, not wanting to live in a manner which she felt beneath her. She was a pretentious, insufferable snob. To his relief, she filed for divorce in order to marry an ancient, wealthy widower who was charmed by her good looks and fine manners. Jacob McIntosh finally could enjoy a freedom he had never known and was looking forward to opening his medical practice in the west.

A few more passengers got down from their wagons and scampered into Wolf's Dry Goods to either purchase items or use the outhouses behind the store.

While Dr. McIntosh and Cadan gathered their belongings, others approached the oxen train. One was Jens the Blacksmith, the other Henry, the proprietor of the Nugget Saloon. The latter had a small load of whiskey, rum and beer to unload and needed help carrying it into his establishment. A rail-thin man stood behind Henry. His clothing hung on him and he appeared too frail to be of much help. Seeing he was needed, Cadan asked, "May I be of assistance sir?"

"Much obliged," Henry answered.

Cadan introduced himself to Henry as did Dr. McIntosh which proved advantageous for all three. The slack jawed, thin man simply turned and shuffled back to the saloon without saying a word.

The mercantile owner, Franz Wolf had a small load of

merchandise to pick up and was anxious to check on the condition of it. Gigantic freight wagons pulled by long lines of brawny mules were used to haul extremely heavy goods. His merchandise included clothing and food which could easily be unloaded. His son, Harold was enlisted to help. He was twelve and filled with energy. Lucy, the wife of Franz as well as their daughter, Lily Ann worked alongside Franz to bring in packages.

Jens, the Blacksmith was there to check on the condition of the animals, harnesses and wagons. He was a Dane and spoke little English. Although married, he and his wife were childless. He had a steady hand and calm demeanor with horses. He observed more than he spoke. By studying a horse's hooves, eyes, teeth and coat, Jens knew dietary habits or even the terrain they lived in. He judged men on how they treated animals as it proved their character. Although somewhat short, he had powerful arms, hands, shoulders and legs. He wore a long leather apron around his waist and his long hair bound by a leather strap. Jens had a furrowed brow and square chin and looked as if he too had been forged out of metal. He resembled a Viking.

Part III

After the men finished helping Henry, he asked if they would like to quench their thirst with drinks on the house. "I don't mind if I do," Cadan said. Dr. McIntosh shook his head in agreement.

The two made their way over to the bar but Henry motioned to one of the tables and said "Sit a spell, gents.

Will it be whiskey, beer, sarsaparilla?"

"Beer thank you," responded Cadan.

"Yes," Dr. McIntosh agreed.

Smiling, Henry placed three clean glasses and a large bottle of beer on the rough-hewn table.

Before his first sip, Cadan spotted a relic of a piano against a back wall he didn't notice when they were moving the crates inside. He pushed his chair back, got up and walked over to it. Henry and Dr. McIntosh noticed the younger man touch the keys with tenderness as one does an old pet.

"Do you know how to play?" Henry asked.

Cadan stuttered as he had a tendency to do when excited saying, "I am a pianist"

"Is that so?" chuckled Henry.

He had heard others claim they were piano players. They boasted about their skill after a few drinks. When their fingers pounded the ivory keys, they couldn't read a note let alone play with feeling or finesse. Naturally, he assumed Cadan wouldn't know how to play either. However, he was soon proven wrong.

Within moments, it was as if they were sitting in a concert hall instead of a saloon. Stephen snuck out of the storeroom and slumped in a chair not far from the piano. They were all enthralled by Cadan's mastery. It was astonishing that the battered upright could sound so magical. After twenty minutes, Cadan walked back to the table, took a few sips of his beer, walked back to the stool and resumed playing for another twenty minutes.

All the while he played Dr. McIntosh, Henry and Stephen sat as if in a spell.

When he stopped playing, he turned around and asked Henry if he could rent a room for the time being as he had no cabin or shanty of his own.

Henry rented rooms upstairs. They were not fancy, but they were clean. He ran a decent saloon, no prostitutes, no dance hall, no cheating at cards, no watered-down liquor, honest gambling or deal with the law. Deadwood was not far away if they needed more excitement. He did not want his patrons to fight and if he sensed one brewing made certain they took it outside.

For the next week, Cadan spent time acclimating to his new surroundings. He began by asking questions at the assay office and establishing an account at the long, narrow, low-roofed log structure that served as a bank. The building was dominated by a huge, impenetrable vault which sat at the back. There was one window with steel bars across it, a thick oak door and a desk for the banker. A hardened face guard stood next to the vault with a shotgun. He had the look of an outlaw. Cadan had never seen such a rudimentary building serve as a bank but it was Credence, not London. He enjoyed visiting miners who came in to "wet their whistles" each night in the Nugget. His gift at the piano gave the plain little saloon a certain ambiance that was unheard of in such a place. With his amiable manner, magnificent piano playing and stuttering speech, it always put others at ease. He was able to file a claim within a week. He never disclosed he was the illegitimate grandson of one of the most powerful men in England which was prudent. All one could see was a decent fellow and a young greenhorn. Though he had generations of Cornwall miners in his blood, mining would prove to be far more difficult than he ever imagined.

Denis Moreau

M'en revenant de la jolie Rochelle,
M'en revenant de la jolie Rochelle,
J'ai rencontré trois jolies demoiselles.
C'est l'aviron qui nous mène, qui nous mène,
C'est l'aviron qui nous mène en haut.

Denis spoke little, but his rich baritone voice could be heard singing as he worked splitting logs behind his small dwelling along the ridge. He sang when he was happy which was seldom, and he sang when he was heartbroken, which was often. His songs ranged from wind and weather to love and loss. Sometimes he sang of the seasons or even beautiful women, but he always sang.

He was the son of a French-Canadian Voyageur and Ojibwe mother. He was raised near the Snake River post in Minnesota. Denis witnessed the end of an era, that of the powerful American Fur Trade which was the livelihood of not only his father, but grandfather. His French father taught him to play a fiddle and his maternal grandfather, an Ojibwe flute. Denis could hear music echo through the trees, birds and wind which was nature's chorus. He learned to trap and hunt as well as speak three languages: French, English and his mother's native tongue. As a small child he listened to the stories of bygone rendezvous' and mountains to the far west. He was a fascinating mix of Ojibwe skills, French sensitivity, Catholicism and native beliefs.

He was married in his late teens to a sweet natured Ojibwe girl he had known and loved his whole life. They had a small son they cherished. Denis had all he could ask for and was a content man until he returned from a hunting trip to find his cabin burned to the ground. Nothing was left but ashes, including his beautiful young wife and little boy.

There were no witnesses as they lived some distance from any settlements. Had it been an accident or murder? Half crazed and in shock, he said goodbye to his aging parents and the life he once knew and loved. His grief pushed him west hoping to ease the horrific images or at least come to terms with it somehow.

With nobody to look after, Denis set his sights on the Black Hills. Crossing the "Missoura" as he called it, he brought hardened, unmatched tracking and survival skills. He was known to be reclusive and seldom smiled. But his melodious voice could be heard singing the French canoe songs of his father. His father also taught him to pray Catholic prayers that he muttered quietly for he didn't want anyone to hear his lamentations. He vehemently protected his privacy. A dutiful son, he would send his parents a letter once a month. Denis Moreau toiled long hours in his placer mine which helped him work through his darkest periods, in turn, saving his sanity. Still, the faces and voices of his wife and child were frequent visitors in his sweet dreams as well as cruel nightmares. Denis lived in a purgatory of his own. Their ghosts were his constant companions and never strayed far from his daily routine, thus keeping him company.

He was a handsome man, just twenty-six years old with premature silver streaks in his black hair and beard. His burnished skin was a gift of his mother and his blue-grey eyes, his father. He wore his thick long hair in a queue and sometimes wore a blue toque on his head. Medium height, he was sinewy and strong. He wore a Hudson Bay capote, red sash around his waist and leathers in winter. He was used to wearing both moccasins and boots but stopped wearing the moccasins once he began working in the mine.

When he first settled in Credence, his dealings with others were distant but polite. Still, he found himself longing more for human company which was only natural.

He would watch his fellow miners sit around a glowing campfire while the Irishman, Ginger Fitz, played his fiddle. Other miners played accompaniment on their instruments. Denis was taken with the cacophony of sounds made up by a small concertina, penny whistle, crude skin drum called a bodhran a Scotsman played and even a Jew Harp. Sometimes Ginger would break out in song adding to the merriment. Ginger did not possess a voice for singing and knew it. Yet he could whistle like a bird which was a delight. He would only sing long enough for the group to find their voices drowning out his pitiful voice. He was always relieved when their voices took over and he could concentrate on his fiddle playing. Ginger's main strength was knowing his limitations.

Morose moods of the miners usually lifted with some stomping their feet or dancing a rollicking wild Irish jig. Yet, other times they were subdued listening to the woeful sounds of the fiddle. Each man had his own story. Some were filled with love. success and adventure. Others were filled with deep sorrow like Denis. They were the broken ones.

The men's faces were a mix of mirth, disappointment or weariness. It was not unusual to see tears in some of their eyes or heads lowered hiding their grief. For many had lived hard lives before coming to Credence. Denis was not the only one who suffered in silence. However, the group found comfort and comradery with one another. Seldom did they argue, but if they did, it was settled before they turned in for the night. A few took deep draughts out of small whiskey jugs, others refrained from drinking, preferring to live a clean, sober life.

The bright red-orange flames lit the circle of men. From his perch, Denis could see their glowing faces and hear the uproarious tunes of Ginger's fiddle. One night longing for company, Denis showed up with his flute and powerful singing voice. It was the beginning of a new life and life-long friendship between Denis and Ginger.

Part II

By October, many of the miners had struck it rich. Denis was no exception. His hard work all summer and fall paid off leaving him a hefty sum safely tucked in the Credence Bank vault. His frugal nature kept him from squandering it on gambling tables, drink or soiled doves in Deadwood. He had no taste for vices. However, he did have an interest in the beautiful widow who lived below his hilltop dwelling. He had an unobstructed view of her back yard where he often saw her busy at work each morning before he headed to his mine.

Her name was Klara Eriksson. She was a Swedish immigrant, tall with thick yellow hair she wore in a neat rolled braid. But it was her striking blue eyes that one noticed immediately. They were the color of the sky.

She walked with dignity with her head held high and shoulders back as if steadying herself against hardships she may yet face.

Klara ran a tiny hotel. It was clean and provided hearty meals. She had a vegetable garden in the back with beans, onions, squash, corn, carrots, cabbage and pumpkins. Under the kitchen window a small flower and herb bed thrived.

She did both the work of a man and woman after her husband died of appendicitis. She not only took care of her little girl, Sofia, but milked the cow, collected the eggs, tended the garden, hauled water, sewed clothes, ironed, cooked, baked, mended the fence and took in boarders from morning until late into the evening.

It was not as if the many men in the settlement didn't offer to help for many did and often. She simply was uneasy around them and remained aloof. Her cold demeanor was her defense.

Denis had never seen such a woman. He found her fascinating and courageous. Yet, he was acutely aware of the dangers and difficulties the world posed for a mother and her child. How exhausted she must be he thought to himself. He decided to keep watch over Klara and little

Sofia. He knew he would never see his beloved wife and little boy again and he longed for them. However, he was not certain if he could go through the rest of his life without someone to share it with.

As the days grew chillier, Klara would find fresh deer meat, elk or wild turkey on her doorstep which had already been cleaned and dressed. One time she found an extremely large and valuable white wolf fur blanket. She never found out who the benefactor was. But she wondered if it was the French Canadian, Denis. There was little doubt he was the best hunter in Credence. He was also the only one who could read sign and track both animal and man. He enjoyed hunting elk, deer, wild turkey and fishing the stream that flowed through the settlement. He would say to other hunters "Keep your nose open," a reminder to always be on alert. Bears and cougars roamed the hills and it could spell danger. But Denis also meant Sioux and Cheyenne for they had been lied to and betrayed. He respected and understood the natural world far more than mankind. He would often walk by her little hotel/restaurant on the way to Wolf's, smile and nod at her. She wanted to ask him if he was the one who generously provided game and gifted her with such a luxurious fur blanket. However, she felt it would make her appear forward.

Before long, it became his morning habit to look down at her back yard in hope of seeing her if just for a moment. He knew her routine of collecting eggs, milking her cow or tending her productive garden. Somehow, it gave him comfort seeing her busy at her daily tasks. He admired her not only for her fine looks, but also industry and determination. One morning he noticed something he had never witnessed before. Klara was on her knees bent over her pumpkin patch with her head buried in her hands.

He could not determine if she was hurt. Thoughts of his deceased family flashed through his brain. Dropping the coffee pot, he scrambled down the ridge to assist her. When he got to her side a startled Klara jumped to her feet and took a step back. She seemed embarrassed at the sight of Denis. He asked, "Are you hurt?"

She shook her head no and wiped her tear stained face with her apron. Then she pointed to what had been a thriving pumpkin patch. A pestilence of some sort destroyed it during the night, leaving only one perfectly formed tiny pumpkin. Seeing the last perfectly formed little pumpkin reminded her of her infant son she lost on the journey out west. Her beautiful little baby was buried hundreds of miles away, with only a makeshift cross to mark his grave. The wagon train could not linger and slowly resumed the long journey. Klara, her husband and little Sofia caught up to it after a few hours. Klara sat alone in the back of the wagon her eyes glued to the spot where her baby was buried until it vanished from sight. Her arms ached to hold him just once more, kiss his plump cheeks and nurse him at her breast. It troubled her greatly knowing he was left behind alone an unprotected from the wild. A part of her died that day, but she still had Sofia and her husband. She clung to hope that no harm would come to either of them.

The young widow had suffered too many losses. It was a heartbreaking burden Denis understood all too well and so he stood quietly by her side. He felt awkward because he had no words of comfort Yet, his presence was enough. Without speaking, they drew strength from one another and shared their common bond of great loss.

He decided the placer mine could wait that day and helped Klara instead with her chores. He cleared away the area leaving only a neat brown patch of earth for next spring's planting. He asked where the tools were so he could straighten and fix fence posts, hammer loose nails and clean the cow pen. It gave Klara a chance to gather herself. Doing the simple tasks helped them both and before long Klara said, "Would you like to share supper with us this evening?"

"I would be honored, Mrs. Eriksson," was all he spoke.

When Klara opened the door, she did not recognize the scrubbed, clean shaven, and well-groomed gentleman at her door. Little Sofia hid behind her mother, too bashful to speak. Denis Moreau had transformed into a handsome frontiersman instead of a wild recluse known to sing at all hours of day and night.

♫ ♪ ♫

The Nugget's Philosopher & Soldier

Ginger

Slight, about 5'4", wearing a mass of unruly, red hair and long, tangled beard, Thomas Fitzgerald resembled a leprechaun to many. He was far younger than he looked which he knew worked in his favor. It gave him the appearance of an eccentric, down on his luck miner. Ginger, as he was better known, was blessed with a brilliant, quick wit and unceasing love of storytelling. He also possessed a wild, fiery temper when provoked and firmly believed in banshees and little people.

Ginger was a native of County Cavan Ireland with dreams of striking it rich in America. Indeed, industrious, wily, Ginger was already a wealthy man. He knew how to mine gold and had an uncanny ability to find it along Black Hills creeks. The sand and gravel seemed to shimmer under his feet. He never boasted, nor did he disclose his findings to anyone. His worn, frayed boots and sweat-stained shirts and pants disguised his wealth which was stored safely in the vault in Credence, Deadwood and some sent back east by a treasure coach. He never boasted of his success to his fellow miners which was wise. For even friends can become envious or scheme when it came to gold. If asked about his mines, he would put his head down, shake it and say in his most pitiful voice, "Luck is not with me lad," or "My pot of gold is just waiting." He was clever at hiding nuggets from everyone and always worked alone. His senses were always on guard for sounds of footsteps approaching so he could protect his discoveries. He knew how to place twigs or branches in such a way that alerted him should someone be getting too close. Like his outward appearance, his area was messy. However, it was simply an ingenious ruse. Overturned rocks and debris littered his work area along the creek. To an onlooker it appeared poor Ginger was desperate and frantically searching anywhere for a bit of gold. However, the whole area hid small pockets that could be filled with nuggets or gold sand should one get near. Even his filthy clothing hid fine gold dust that he shook out inside his pathetic shanty each night with the door locked and window covered by a tarp. He wore a certain set of work clothes to mine and was careful to brush tiny fragment of gold dust out before being seen. He wore other frayed pants, shirts and coat when he was in the Nugget or bought goods at Wolf's. He washed his work clothes himself back of his shack in a galvanized tub. People thought he was too cheap or poor to pay the local laundress when in fact he was simply being wise. When it was time for him to leave for the day, he would scout his area making certain nobody was nearby.

Satisfied, he would quickly scoop out nuggets or fine gold sand and place it in bags under his shovel, pick, canteen or in a leather satchel tucked tightly under his steady burro's blanket. He was extremely cautious about his tidy technique. He did not wish to spill gold from the bags. Clever Ginger knew enough to always have just enough gold to pay for his needs and in doing so offset suspicion. He may well have been a bit of leprechaun after all.

Thomas Fitzgerald had known poverty, famine and despair in Ireland. He hated England as did all of those who suffered at their rule. He was a good, loyal son to his mother and begged her and his younger sister to join him in America, the land of promise and freedom. But they refused which was understandable. The emerald isle was their home and a thousand years of his ancestors. Nevertheless, Ginger always sent large sums home which lifted them out of their sad conditions; thus, providing security and comfort. He knew one day he would return to his homeland, perhaps finding an Irish girl to marry. But, for the time being his attention was amassing a fortune which he knew impossible in Ireland.

Ginger was not greedy and felt each man deserved his fair share of what the mountains held. If they toiled unceasingly, they deserved rewards. Like him, they too may have built up stores of wealth hidden in unknown vaults. It was their business just as it was his business.

Ginger loved to share stories of Ireland, play his worn old fiddle and fife and enjoy a beer or shot of whiskey. Wise to a fault, he never drank more than he could handle knowing too much drink caused the lips to say things one later regretted. He always looked less cunning than he was and always seemed more inebriated than he was. A master of disguise, he had everyone fooled which worked in his favor.

He had habit of quoting Marcus Aurelius when something amused, perplexed or brought him close to tears. His favorite saying was: "Each day promises its own gifts." With each new day, the little Irishman blessed himself, said his prayers, and lived the quote of a Roman Emperor born thousands of years ago.

Stephen

Stephen slumped in a chair all skin and bones. In a sense, he was a Civil War casualty. The haunted soldier spent most days in the Nugget trying to erase images he carried with him of the carnage of a distant battlefield. Cannon balls blasted inside his head while bayonets lanced his heart. Stephen carried bits and pieces of shrapnel in his mind rather than inside his body. How he ended up in the mining settlement of Credence was a mystery. He showed up one cold, misty morning at the back door of the Nugget, shivering and looking for work.

All anybody knew of him was his name and that he grew up on a small farm in the state of Illinois. Now and then he would talk of his little brother, Daniel, who followed him into war and never came home. When Stephen slept, which was seldom, he dreamt of his childhood playing in his father's farm fields with his younger brother chasing after him. Running, always running, Daniel never stopped running to catch up to his older brother, Stephen.

Daniel hero worshipped his old brother from babyhood. He followed him everywhere and hung on to every word his older brother spoke. When Stephen enlisted so did Daniel. One day he simply took off without his widowed mother's permission, lied about his age and soon was marching into battle like his brother, Stephen. It crushed his mother as Daniel was her favorite. He had been a sweet, loving child with merry eyes and a ready smile. He loved to laugh unlike his serious older brother who smiled seldom and found little humor in anything.

One day Stephen received a letter from his distraught mother regarding Daniel's safety. He had no idea his little brother enlisted which was true and wrote his mother back stating he would do what he could to locate the whereabouts of Daniel. More than anything he wanted to get him home safely. But, as hard as he tried, he never found the brigade he was in. Stephen was more concerned about his brother's safety than his own. He loved his little brother deeply and felt the impressionable fourteen-year old was living in horror because of him. Months passed, bloody battles and skirmishes waged on, and still he did not know if Daniel was safe, or even alive. His greatest hope was Daniel deserted as many others did and somehow be pardoned because of his age.

On a bright, cloudless day, Stephen was assigned duty with the burial detail. It was a grim task no soldier ever wanted. Battle grounds were scenes of carnage, always the stuff of nightmares. Faces showing expressions of grimacing pain, terror or sorrow on fellow soldiers would forever be seared in the minds of those on burial duty. The senses alone were assaulted so harsh were the scenes they dealt with. Sometimes bodies lay for days, unattended, at the mercy of nature, scavenging birds or beasts.

With the others, Stephen went about his dour task of burying soldiers, many were placed in common graves. It was a hideous reminder of how fragile human beings with their torn limbs and body parts strewn across bloodied battlefields. It shocked and revolted them. Still, they worked on. They understood they owed it to their fellow soldiers who were taken so violently in the line of duty, honor and sacrifice.

By midafternoon, they came to what had been a very beautiful ridge. It seemed almost in the clouds with a view that went on for miles and miles. They noticed a torn Union flag waving eerily in the breeze at the very top and decided to make their way over to it. Getting closer, they saw the flag bearer, face down, still gripping it valiantly. Lucky in a sense, Stephen thought, as he noticed carrion birds above the bodies of the dead, circling, landing and pecking their faces and eyes. He hated the vile creatures. Stephen and the others took off their coats and swung wildly at them. At least it scared them away for the time being.

As he and the others bent over to remove the flag from the lifeless hand, Stephen knew without turning him over, it was his beloved younger brother Daniel. He fell to his knees, turned his little brother over and brushed the mud and blood off his once young and cheerful face. The others were silent as they saw Stephen rocking the stiff, lifeless young boy in his arms, weeping and talking in hushed tones ...

Without looking at his fellow soldiers, Stephen placed Daniel in his coat, picked him up in his arms and walked away from the bloodied place. They knew, it was Stephen's little brother he talked endlessly about.

Stephen walked as far as he could with Daniel in his arms, picking his way through the scores of dead Union and Confederate soldiers. He trudged on. A few times he stumbled, gathered his brother back in his arms and continued down the ridge with the body of his brother searching for a spot to bury him with some semblance of dignity. After quite some time, he spotted a few majestic oak trees in the draw. Reaching them he placed Daniel on the ground, cleaned his brother's uniform the best he could with his hands, took off Daniel's hat and swept the brown hair from his rigid, lifeless face. It was a painful thing for the others to witness as they followed their comrade not sure what he was doing. Stephen started digging a grave, under one of the trees. They could hear him muttering to himself the whole time, as if his brother could hear him. But he knew Daniel's merry eyes would never shine again for anyone, nor would his infectious laugh be heard except for angels. More than anything, he wished he had died instead of Daniel.

He was exhausted and struggled with the shovel. He was all out with the dreadful day let alone carrying his brother's lifeless body down the ridge while toting a shovel. He heard a fellow solider say, "Stephen, we can do the rest." While they dug, Stephen took out his small knife he carried and carved his brother's initials, birth date and death date in the side of the oak Daniel was placed near. His little brother would forever be far from his home in Illinois.

Stephen was never the same after that. He was deemed mentally unfit to continue. He wrote his mother telling her what had happened. She died soon after. Riddled with guilt,

Stephen was slowly working on killing himself from drink and neglect.

If not for the kind saloon owner, Henry, he would not have a roof over his head, a place to sleep, or a bite to eat. He reminded Henry of one of the stray cats that jump off wagons while passing through town. Lost or frightened, the cats always found themselves at the back door of the Nugget sipping milk, getting scraps to eat and a safe, warm place to hide.

♬ ♫ ♫

Lily Ann & Lucy

Part I

Her name was Lily Ann. Like her name, she was sweet and untouched. She was the daughter of Franz Wolf and his wife, Lucy. She was not the most beautiful girl Cadan had ever seen, but there was something different about her that captivated him. He was smitten with her from the moment they exchanged words in her father's mercantile.

Her parents, Franz and Lucy kept close watch over her which was understandable. Mining settlements had few women, and a pretty sixteen-year old was a prize.

Lily Ann was both dutiful daughter and kind older sister to her younger brother, Harold. She worked alongside her mother each day in the store and home rather than sit idly looking in the Montgomery Ward mail order catalog.

Her silky auburn hair hung down her back like red-gold flames held only by a ribbon. She wore a different color each day of the week adding to her girlish charm. Cadan found the freckles that dotted her nose playful and her green eyes unique. Her mouth was shaped like a heart, and when she favored him with a smile, his world was a better place. To her credit she was a modest girl preferring to hide her voluptuous figure in calico or gingham dresses.

Lily Ann had no idea how lovely she was. Her parents instilled values in her which had nothing to do with her outward appearance. They did not spoil her even though they could afford it. In turn, it gave her a sense of confidence and self-worth not dependent upon beauty. She was intelligent, kind and sensitive. Franz and Lucy wanted both Lily Ann and Harold to be capable of taking care of themselves. They knew the world could be a dangerous and inhospitable place. That meant studying math, science, history and reading the classics. Franz was determined his children would not be "dolts" but they still enjoyed a healthy balance of work, play and study.

One day Cadan noticed Lily Ann standing alone in the doorway of her father's store and walked over. Wanting to impress her, he recited the first line from *"A Red, Red Rose"* by Robert Burns without stuttering.

"O, my love is like a red, red rose
 That's newly sprung in June"...

Before he began the next line, Lily Ann answered him.

"O my love is like a melody
 That's sweetly played in tune"...

Smiling at one another they recited the remainder of the poem in unison.

From behind the counter, Franz and Lucy exchanged a knowing smile. It was easy to recognize the budding courtship between their daughter and young Mr. Gray. As summer was gently slipping into fall, the young man became their number one customer.

Part II
Lucy's Story

Lucy was a fine wife and loving mother who lived an exemplary life. However, she had a secret, a tawdry and sinful past.

She was a mail order bride that proved to be not only healthy and good looking but hard working and loyal. Franz was a happy man to have such a wife and Lucy grew to love Franz. They carved out a good life together and seldom, if ever, raised their voices to one another. Lucy was grateful to escape her past and Franz was pleased to have an obedient, lady-like spouse and doting mother to his children.

Franz, Lily Ann and Harold were her life. Each day she could be found behind the counter at Wolf's Dry Goods alongside Franz. Lily Ann and Harry had daily chores and school lessons. Credence did not yet have a teacher so both Lucy and Franz took it upon themselves to provide what education they could and ordered a small library size collection of books from catalogs. Franz often read from an old Bible that once belonged to his German grandfather. Lucy loved it as much as her children. She felt a sense of peace hearing of the trials and tribulations of the people in the Old Testament and New Testament. The word of God gave her hope and peace. Each night, she sought heavenly forgiveness in silent prayers for things that occurred long ago. Likewise, each Sunday the little family attended church services in the tiny dwelling of the Lutheran minister.

Franz had a quick mind for numbers and enjoyed teaching his children arithmetic, especially complicated equations. He wanted Harry to follow in his footsteps, perhaps even run a store of his own one day. An enterprising man, Franz was going to open another Mercantile in Deadwood before long.

Lily Ann, unlike her brother Harold, had no mind for business. Rather, she loved reading novels and poetry and often read aloud to her parents. She loved to sew, embroider, cook and bake. Although not vain, she had self-worth and was fastidious in her appearance. Because she possessed bright white teeth and a fetching smile, she had no intention of visiting the would-be dentist whose shutter hung outside the back stairs of the Nugget. She watched as many of his unsuspecting patients left his office in acute pain and distress. Some of them would come into the store asking for pain killers while others drowned out the throbbing pain in the Nugget.

To the casual observer, the Wolf family lived an enviable life compared to most. In a sense, they did. They loved one another deeply which by any measure is wealth enough.

Lucy was almost certain her past would not find her in the small settlement. Yet her mind was troubled from time to time, should anyone find out about her hard life prior to meeting Franz. She was a victim of circumstance no doubt, but others might feel differently should they discover her sullied past. Indeed, she spent a great deal of time praying Franz and her beloved children would never know. When any of them asked about her childhood she simply told them she was orphaned at a young age and had to work as a domestic before meeting Franz. It was half true, half lie.

Seventeen years ago, she fled a life with no future. When she saw mail order bride ads to go west, she promptly wrote back to one written by Franz. He sent a small photo of himself and she liked what she saw. He had an intelligent, kind and solid appearance. She answered truthfully about her age, height, weight, and appearance. What she did not disclose was the fact she worked in a St. Louis saloon as a dance hall girl whose sole purpose was to entice men to drink, gamble or go upstairs to the brothel. Her job was to separate a man from his money. She was the bait, which in a sense kept her from being "ruined" like the girls upstairs, although her job was far more devious. She drew admiring glances, but no one was allowed more than a dance with her. Her good looks and ability to shuffle cards were window dressing that never posed a problem, until one night a nondescript looking patron wanted more from her than her bright smile. The man was an out of control mean drunk. For some unknown reason he focused his discontent on her. He peered at her while she shuffled cards for the men at the poker table. Lucy wore a provocative ruffled bodice midnight blue dress. It was designed to show a woman's figure. Her hair was in disarray from dancing. Men took notice of her no doubt that evening.

To the enraged drunk, she was asking for trouble with her bold appearance. He eventually pushed through the loud, crowded smoke-filled room, intent on dragging her upstairs. Lucy was unaware of the man approaching her as she sat at the poker table. Stumbling up to the table the drunken man shouted in a slurred voice "You're coming with me." Then, he tipped over the table, upsetting cards, poker chips and spilling drinks. The poker players quickly scrambled from their chairs, one reached for his gun but thought better of pulling it should Lucy get shot. Before anyone could stop the deranged man, he slapped her hard across her cheek, leaving an ugly red imprint. Pulling her by the arm, he half dragged, half threw her towards the stairs. Her dress was ripped at the bodice, half exposing her breasts. Ashamed and terrified, Lucy screamed! She tried to flee while holding up the shredded ruffled bodice. It was an outrageous, obscene scene. She knew what would happen if he got her alone upstairs or in the back alley. Some of the bystanders tried to intervene, but when the weasel faced drunk flashed his knife, they stood back. They liked the pretty girl named Lucy, but they were not willing to risk their life, or end up disfigured. Her job came with risks. After all, she put herself in harm's way by working in such a place, many felt. Just then, a giant named Pete who stood nearly six feet-seven stood in front of the stairs. In a calm, deep voice he said, "Let her go."

The drunk laughed and lunged with his knife, just missing Pete's stomach. But Pete was fast. He stepped aside, just missing the wicked blade and grabbed the drunk's hand, forcing the knife out. Pete kicked it across the floor, well out of the drunk's reach. Seeing his plan foiled, the drunk spat a filthy mix of chewing tobacco and whiskey on Pete's shirt. It proved to be the weasel faced man's last mistake. Enraged and disgusted, Pete punched the drunk in the nose violently with his mallet of a fist. The drunk crashed to the sawdust floor. The room fell silent. The bartender ran over to a stunned Lucy.

A few patrons knelt to revive the drunk by shaking and slapping his face. "He's not coming around!" one bystander said.

"Look at his face, what happened to his nose? It's not where it's supposed to be!" said another from the group standing nearby.

"But, it was only one punch!" could be heard from the back of the room. It appeared Pete's enormous fist shoved the man's nose directly into the drunk's brain, causing instant death!

Not long after, Pete was taken away to stand trial for murder even though it was not his intention to kill the despicable man. He only wanted to save Lucy.

Her life had been a series of horrible misfortunes starting at the age of five. Her earliest memories were vague and heartbreaking. She remembered always being cold, having little to eat and strangers taking her mother's body away. She had no family, which meant living in a wretched charity home for orphans. There she learned to survive. Lucy, like so many other unfortunates, struggled each day with terror and despair.

At the age of fourteen and with nobody to cling to, Lucy ended up in the sordid saloon. There she got fed and was provided a small room in the back of the building with a lock. The lock kept unwanted visitors out. What little money she had went towards a few cheap colorful dresses, a brush, mirror and comb of her own, a wool blanket and a pair of good shoes. She longed for a new pair as a child. The shoes were her only luxury.

The bartender treated her kindly realizing she deserved much better, but the owner looked at her as one looks at livestock. He assessed all his "girls" in the same demeaning manner. He lusted for her as did the patrons, but he did not wish to "soil" the goods, at least for a little while. For the time being she was his main attraction.

He was a bald, greasy, middle aged man who reveled in wearing ridiculous and flamboyant clothing. His flabby lips were red as if he wore some of the makeup of the soiled doves trapped upstairs. His soft pudgy fingers were filled with clusters of diamond rings. His bulging, vacant eyes like those of a fish, added to his overall repulsiveness.

He was confident that there would always be another poverty- stricken girl down on her luck with no resources. He held a perverse, immoral nature. It amused him how naïve girls were when they walked into his saloon for the first time, some barely thirteen, and how haggard they were when they walked out for the last time, some, not even thirty. They all resembled forlorn old alley cats. Worse yet, many died from neglect, disease or their own hand.

Lucy felt great pity for the girls upstairs. She saw their tear-stained faces and heard their weeping. It saddened and disgusted her what they were forced to do in order to survive. She realized once they were no longer attractive, or became ill, they would be cast out like garbage. It was only a matter of time for her as well. Eventually the saloon owner would discover a younger, fresh faced girl to work as bait for the patrons. She would be doomed if she didn't act immediately to alter her fate.

A couple weeks after the incident, she was overjoyed to find another letter informing her all travel expenses were paid in full by the German, Franz Wolf. She would become his mail order bride. Lucy vowed to make the best of it, even if she couldn't speak a word of German.

Part III
The Preacher

On a cool autumn morning, a man rode into Credence on a tall dark gray gelding. He wore a white cleric collar in stark contrast to his black coat, boots and pants. He wore a wide brimmed black hat shielding his eyes. His silver hair was shoulder length and he was clean shaven. But it was his size that one took notice of more than anything. He was a big man.

His name was Pastor Peter Stewart, a Methodist Circuit Rider or "Saddlebag Preacher." He carried only what he could fit in his saddlebags. He spread God's message in mining camps, fields, settlements, shanties, cabins, dugouts and saloons. Pete was assigned to travel a certain area or circuit every year and needed a few provisions for his journey. His life was not a comfortable one. Sometimes he found himself in dark, dirty, uncomfortable surroundings preaching to those who were lost, debased and hardened by life. Some people and places he came across were dangerous, but he was unafraid. Many were miserable sinners. Others were victims of poverty or injustice. Most were simply sheep without a shepherd. He traveled from one settlement to another preaching God's word. It was his calling after serving ten years in a Missouri prison for taking the life of another man with his fist, although it was an accident. Within the prison walls he spent his waking hours studying the Bible. He made a vow to help others one day that had fallen on hard times, lost their faith, or never had any to begin with. Pete knew both sorrow and joy. The west had a desperate need for such preachers and John Wesley's message to save as many souls as you can resonated with Pete. He was a perfect fit, one who could share his own story of faith with those who faltered. He never judged anyone and could be trusted with those who shared their own stories of brokenness. He was well liked and respected. He was a single man in his 40s, older than most circuit preachers. The truth of the matter was, he fell in love with a beautiful young woman but never told her. He never could find the words, so remained silent. Ironically, he became a powerful orator only after finding his calling. He still thought of the young woman from time to time and prayed she found joy in her life, for she desperately needed it. His congregation was spread hundreds of miles apart. Pete did not have a church building to conduct Sunday service. But he had the ability to change the hearts of those who heard his words. He was filled with what one could only call the grace of God. He always began his sermons with, "Behold the Lamb of God, that taketh away the sins of the world." He was there for those who seemed beyond repair and beyond redemption. He was a beacon of hope.

He was recently assigned a new area after serving in and around Deadwood and remote northern regions. Pete knew the small settlement of Credence already had a Lutheran minister residing there. Therefore, he always rode around the settlement rather than stop. But on that autumn day he needed to purchase a pound of coffee and so he tied his horse in front of Wolf's Dry Goods, walked up the steps and opened the door.

Lucy was on a ladder stacking wool garments and blankets when the little bell announced a customer entered the store. Franz was behind the counter and greeted Pete with "Good morning sir."

Preacher Pete smiled and said, "I need a pound of coffee please." Pete had a sweet tooth and after seeing the jars of brightly colored candy added, "I would like a pound of lemon drops, rock candy and a few peppermints if you don't mind." All he could afford on his miniscule salary was a pound.

Lucy, came down from the ladder, straightened her apron and walked to the counter where Pete stood. She was taken by the man's height at first, as he towered over Franz. Then she recalled the giant who stepped in to save her from the drunken weasel, what seemed a lifetime ago. Looking up at Pete, her heart went numb.

Pastor Pete looked at the attractive woman with the auburn hair and beautiful smile and remembered.

The little bell rang once again as another customer walked in, this time a local miner. "Lucy, can you help the minister?"

Lucy, in shock, was silent. She did not hear her husband's request.

Franz repeated himself, "Lucy, help the reverend while I take care of this customer."

She could only squeak out, "Yes" to Franz.

Standing across from each other at the counter, Pete and Lucy looked into each other's eyes. They were transported to a painful time and place they both wished to forget. Lucy's face had a blank look of terror. Pete knew why and understood. He glanced over his shoulder and saw Franz immersed in conversation with the other customer. He was too busy to notice his wife's face and shaking hands.

Pete gently placed his enormous hand on hers, noticed the wide gold wedding band, smiled at her warmly, and whispered "I am happy for you Lucy. God bless you."

Her troubled eyes suddenly filled with relief. She was speechless. She knew her past would remain where it belonged, in the past.

Pastor Pete turned and walked over to Franz and the miner who were discussing the growth of Deadwood, which gave her a chance to compose herself and fill his order. Pete shielded her then as he did so many years ago.

In a few minutes the packages were on the counter. Pete paid Franz. As he opened the door to leave, he turned, tipped his hat and thanked them. Franz, Lucy and the miner watched as the big man mounted his tall gray gelding.

"What a mountain of man that preacher is," Franz said as he watched him slowly ride out of Credence.

"Don't you know who he is? That's Pastor Peter" the customer said. "He's as good as his word. I heard his sermon one Sunday morning in a Deadwood saloon a year ago. It gave me goosebumps, made me a believer."

"I wonder where he is off to now?" Franz said.

"No one knows. He just goes where God tells him I reckon," the miner answered.

Lucy remained quiet throughout the exchange. She had a faraway expression on her face, a peaceful look.

After the miner left, Franz glanced at Lucy. It struck him she never looked more beautiful than she did at that moment.

Seeing the devotion in his eyes, Lucy walked over to where her husband stood, took his right hand, and put it on her face where she had been struck so violently seventeen years ago. In a hushed tone, she spoke "Oh, how I love you, Franz. You have given me nothing but joy."

He placed his arm around her and drew her close. Neither spoke a word for a few minutes. Finally, Franz looked at her, winked and said, "Those packages were larger than a pound of coffee and candy. His journey can't be easy and it's getting colder outside. We have so much Lucy. The preacher does God's work. If we could lessen his burden and make it more pleasant for just a little while, it's the least we could do."

"I knew he wouldn't accept charity being a proud man," she replied softly.

Hours later, Pete stopped to make camp along a trickling creek. He was hungry and weary. Before unsaddling his gelding, he removed the saddlebags containing his provisions and the packages he purchased at Wolf's store and placed them on the ground. He thought it odd the packages containing coffee and candy were cumbersome. After making a fire and seeing to the needs of his horse, it was time to prepare a small meal. He opened one of the packages and discovered it contained three pounds of the finer quality candy as well as three pounds of coffee. He knew he only paid for one pound of coffee and a pound of penny candy and thought Lucy had made a mistake as she was so flustered. "What could the other package possibly contain?" he thought.

Nestled in tissue paper were a richly woven black woolen scarf and matching gloves stamped extra-large and one of the colorful woolen blankets Lucy was stacking on the shelves. He shook his head and said to himself "Oh Lucy. I see you're still quick at shuffling, only this time with candy, coffee and kindness." Looking up to the vast, beautiful heavens, he said "Lord you truly work in mysterious ways. Thank you."

Lucy never shared her sorrowful past with Franz. It would only serve to destroy him and their children. For that matter, not a soul that ever lived, or even passed through Credence discovered it. Only God, the preacher and Lucy were in cahoots.

Part IV

On August 15, 1875, an enormous freight wagon bearing the piano arrived. It was covered with blankets to keep it from being scratched or scuffed. In elaborate gold letters it was stamped: Gillow & Company, Lancester, England, a very old and renowned furniture maker. The piano was a Broadwood Cottage style Upright, easily the price of a new home. Its extensively carved legs, molding and trim were fine and impressive. Made of solid straight grain mahogany, its hand painted panels ran across the front and told ancient Greek myths. One was Pan teaching Apollo, another of Mercury, as well as other Greek Gods. It weighed at least 820 pounds. The sheet music holder folded in and out when not in use and could be hidden in the top of the piano when not in use.

It was a curiosity for the little group of citizens watching that day. No one had ever seen such a magnificent instrument before, nor would they again. Except for those working their claims, everyone greeted it. By all measure, nobody had ever seen such a piano. It was extraordinary.

Unloading and moving the piano was a feat itself. A special ramp accompanied it for loading and unloading, but it still demanded manpower.

The piano was too massive to pass through his modest dwelling. In fact, it would have taken up the whole room. The only double doors in Credence were those of Wolf's Dry

Goods. They could accommodate the beautiful piano.

Franz jumped at the opportunity of having the piano sit in his establishment. Music would draw customers and dress up his store at the same time. Besides, he liked the young man and sensed his wife and daughter did too.

Lucy had her own plans for the piano. She viewed it as a kind of match maker for her daughter and Cadan. She felt piano lessons would be necessary for Lily Ann in order to round out her education. Franz agreed thinking what harm could there be as the young couple would be under their noses?

It was settled. Lily Ann would commence music lessons twice a week. She did not mind his stuttering and he did not mind her lack of talent. It could be said, pretty Lily Ann had no musical ability whatsoever. She was both tone deaf and struggled with the notes. However, what she lacked in talent she made up for in enthusiasm. When they sat together at the piano, she preferred looking at his handsome face and strong, tan hands move effortlessly across the keys than the sheet music. Each time their fingers happened to brush up against one another she blushed. One could see, Lily Ann was falling in love.

When he was not working the mine, he spent most of his waking hours in the store playing the piano which everyone enjoyed including the customers. When they saw Cadan at the piano they would request music or songs they liked. Franz liked that because customers often spent more money while listening to the gifted pianist. The only one who was not happy about the piano was Henry. He missed hearing Cadan play on the Nugget's old battered piano.

Cadan's command of the piano had the ability to transport his audience to another place or time. The instrument responded to his touch from a gentle tinkle to a crash of notes. Powerful, passionate, visceral, emotions to delicate, ethereal, tender feelings all blended effortlessly. He took pleasure in accommodating everyone's tastes. Whether they requested a wild, rollicking folk dance or a quiet classical piece by Chopin, he enthralled them. Sometimes he would look up from the keys and see them dancing or heard them humming or singing. His grandfather's gift soon became a gift for the townspeople as well and the centerpiece for social moments in tiny Credence.

Alone in his cabin one evening, Cadan was drawn to music coming from the Nugget Saloon. Seeing him walk through the door, Henry shouted, "Cadan, sit down and play along with the boys." However, he had no intention of playing that night. He missed his family and had a need for company. He just wanted to be in the audience. Cadan smiled warmly and stuttered, "Evening gents," then walked over to the bar railing. He did not want to interrupt their lively rendition of "Old Dan Tucker." Before he could wipe the foam from his upper lip, Ginger Fitz shouted, "Do you think you're too good to play with us, you piano playing fool! Why I bet you could play with one hand and drink with the other! Sit down! Let's hear you play!"

"Just give me a moment to finish," he answered. The group paused for him to get another glass of beer. "Here's to you!" Cadan said as he toasted them. Taking Ginger's challenge, he sat down and played a wild tune with only his left hand while drinking beer with his right. He switched hands every so often. The group cheered. The

Nugget grew louder with drinking and laughter which could be heard not only in the small mining settlement, but far above the black canyon walls and surrounding hills. Cadan couldn't remember the last time he had more fun or made more friends than that night in the Nugget saloon.

♫ ♪ ♫

Tempestuous Deadwood

Franz was ambitious and clever. One could even say he was a bit of a mercenary. There was little he enjoyed more than making money and he was skilled at it. He was always searching for new opportunities. When he heard how money flowed freely in Deadwood, he decided to see for himself.

He devised a plan which on the surface sounded feasible. He would simply hire a manager for the Credence store and start another dry goods in Deadwood. Convincing Lucy and Lily Ann would be his only obstacle. Young Harold was filled with enthusiasm to experience the many mysteries of the sordid gold mining town. However, his beloved wife and daughter wept and pleaded with him to reconsider such a drastic move. But Franz always had the last word and felt they were being hysterical.

At the same time, Cadan was thinking of selling his claim to Ginger Fitzgerald. Although Cadan was an industrious worker, his heart simply was not in it. One year of the back- breaking labor each day was a life-long lesson on how difficult it was to be a miner. He had deep respect for his mother's side of the family in Cornwall. Mining was their livelihood. He was not a snob or "high falutin" he simply knew he was meant for something else. Cadan needed to make his own way and had yet to discover his calling. As a boy he observed Silas manage Glencove for his grandfather, Sir Charles. He learned a great deal about wise decision making that would affect the lives of many. Silas, Gwenna, Sir Charles, his uncles, William and James, all meant the world to him. He missed them more than he thought possible. If not for Lily Ann, he would have sailed back to England before winter.

When Franz asked him if he would manage the store in Credence he agreed. He could live in their quarters upstairs rather than his small wooden dwelling. That way he would be able to play the piano anytime he chose. It was a pleasing prospect except for one thing, Lily Ann would be living in a mining community known for its vice.

When the Wolfs' arrived in Deadwood on a sunny June day, Franz saw for himself that it was a wide open, reckless town. Saloons filled the streets with gambling tables, dancing girls, stage shows, theaters, magicians, boxing matches, free flowing whiskey and all manner of uncouth individuals. The town was filled with prostitutes, some seasoned and extremely foul and evil. Others were young victims lured by lies who became so broken took their lives by hanging, bullet or laudanum. It was a shocking place for one as sweet and gentle as Lily Ann. As for Lucy, the mining town was an ugly reminder of her sad past. It did not take long for Franz to realize his mistake when he noticed the sorrow on both their faces. Mother and daughter knew better than to walk beyond the confines of their store and became prisoners of Franz's greed. He saw that Deadwood was a town that could reward a man with riches or cut them down in various ways. For many, it was a place of broken dreams.

♬ ♪ ♫

February 1877

It was 4" x 2" x 1¼" treasure of sheer delight! Made of gold, silver and enamel, the fancy fern and fleur-de-lis engraved music box was Swiss made and beautifully constructed. After winding a key, a tiny colorful bird fluttered its wings rapidly, twisted its small feathered head from side to side and sang a cheerful song. The little mechanism looked and sounded uncannily real. A perfect Valentine gift, he was intent on delivering it despite the winter weather

He ordered it months in advance and when it finally arrived, it didn't disappoint. Rather than heed the words of others, he set off for Deadwood alone. It wasn't like him to behave in a reckless fashion, but he longed to see Lily Ann after months of separation. He was anxious to see her. He left the care of Wolf's Dry Goods and his beloved piano in the capable hands of the minister and his wife and traveled to Deadwood.

It had been unseasonably warm that February which bode well in his favor. Sunny, warm and with little breeze, he was confident that the short journey would not pose problems. Jens picked out an older, sure-footed, sorrel gelding named Copper for him to ride. Copper didn't spook easily and traveled the rugged wagon worn road to Deadwood many times. The sensible, sturdy sorrel was a perfect traveling companion.

The sunrise was spectacular as he and Copper left Credence. The sky filled with vibrant reds and pinks so bright he had to shield his eyes from their powerful rays. By all accounts it was a glorious day for travel.

He was watchful for hidden dangers that could lurk whether animal, human or weather He looked often at the muddy ground underfoot so Copper wouldn't slip. But the wise horse was not foolish and found his way without guidance, avoiding treacherous, steep areas. With the thaw, the road filled deep wagon ruts with water. Cadan knew bear and cougar lived and roamed the hills and was alert for sounds or sights. Copper relied on his fine sense of smell. It was wise he brought a Colt Peacemaker and 1873 Winchester Repeater rifle just in case. Yet, providence also rode with him that February day so there was no need for either weapon.

By midafternoon it grew exceedingly warm. Most of the snow and ice had melted leaving the primitive road a mess. Hours later he was famished and pulled out the savory food stowed in a saddle bag Klara Moreau prepared for him. It pleased him knowing Klara and Denis were now Mr. and Mrs. Moreau. One could see they were truly happy and little Sofia adored her stepfather. Cadan enjoyed eating his meals there. Suddenly, he thought of his mother and Silas thousands of miles away. He missed them deeply as well as his kind grandfather, Charles as well as his uncles, William and James. He would have many tales to share with all of them some day but for now Cornwall was a world away from the wild hills of Dakota.

Impatiently he peeled off his gloves and stuffed them roughly into his coat pockets, ripping the right liner in the process. He wanted to eat unencumbered. After he sipped a few gulps from the canteen, he took off his coat, rolled it tightly and placed it behind the saddle. He traveled light knowing he would only stay in Deadwood two nights, returning on the third day. He was filled with anticipation. His feelings were real for Lily Ann and he hoped she felt the same.

Surely, it was going to be an early spring he thought as he and Copper entered the gulch and notorious mining town.

Part II

Cadan had seen a great deal of the world compared to many men twice his age. Yet, as he gently nudged Copper to continue through the filthy, cluttered main street of Deadwood, he gawked. Rather than a peaceful, orderly camp like Credence, Deadwood was a vision of unruliness, even violence. The hillsides were littered with dead trees and limbs thus giving the settlement its name. He passed false front buildings, crude shanties, tents, even a few brick buildings which lined the frontier street in search of Wolf's Dry Goods.

He felt concern for the girl he loved. This was no place for her, let alone her family. Passing a saloon, a woman's shrill voice shouted down to him from the balcony above. As he was handsome, she was drawn to him. Startled, he looked up to find her making vulgar, lewd gesture to him advertising her wares. A younger girl standing near the railing looked shamefaced and filled with despair. He pitied her.

He passed Chinese laundries, restaurants, banks, saloons, doctors, dentists, lawyers, liquor stores, an assay office, even bakeries selling dainty confectionaries. It was a throng of activity. A mix of smells permeated the town from pungent, odorous, spicy, savory, to sweet. He noticed more than one sign stating best meal in town 50 cents and a few Butcher shops advertising Vienna sausages, cheese, herring and summer bologna. A few farmers selling chickens, pigs, turnips, and potatoes greeted him as he rode by. Young men and old men walked the streets. Some looked like beggars down on their luck, others arrogant and obviously affluent. Shouting, laughing, coarse language filled the air. He was relieved when he spotted "Wolf's Dry Goods" painted in big, bold, black letters on the side and front of a newly constructed two-story building.

He tied Copper next to the water trough in front of the store, gathered his belongings and entered. Lucy and Franz hearing the bell quickly turned from their tasks and were startled to see him. Elated, Franz shouted at the top of his voice, "Lily Ann, come see who is here!"

"Where is that girl hiding ?" Franz asked Lucy impatiently.

"She's upstairs as usual," Harold answered from the store room where he had been unloading crates. Cadan detected a change in Harold's voice. When he saw Harold, it struck him how much he had grown. He was not such a little boy anymore. Lucy had aged somewhat he detected. Still an extremely attractive woman, her hair had touches of gray and her face bore fine lines. Franz had lost some of his thick curly hair and he appeared somewhat thinner. It seemed Deadwood had not been good for them.

It was true. Lily Ann spent most of her time upstairs, secluded from activity downstairs. She feared Deadwood and hated living there. For that matter, Franz and Lucy had already decided it would be a mistake to remain in such a lawless place and already sold their Deadwood store to another merchant. Franz made a sizable sum in the transaction as the new owner wanted a monopoly on the dry goods business in Deadwood. He was happy to see his competition leave and willing to pay the asking price which was sizeable.

The family was returning to Credence as soon as the new owner took over May 1st. The murder of Wild Bill Hickok, shortly after their arrival the previous summer, as well as thousands of miners, desperados, prostitutes and gamblers coming in droves were concerns. Deadwood had its share of infectious diseases, even smallpox which took a toll on many. The thriving Chinese opium dens had also become part of the fabric of Deadwood. Violence and vice proved too much even for Franz for no amount of wealth was worth his family's safety or peace of mind. He realized nothing was more important to him than his little family.

Shortly after their arrival Lucy and Franz guarded Lily Ann as she soon became a target of unwanted glances, crude remarks, and lust. She was fearful to work downstairs in her parent's store and hid much of the time upstairs where she could not be seen. Until stricter laws were established, it was best to leave. The only one who liked Deadwood was Harold. He enjoyed the excitement and reveled in the wildness of the mining camp much to the dismay of his parents. It was time they left before something disastrous took place. He hero worshipped some of the more shady and colorful citizens of the town as boys tend to do.

When Lily Ann quietly stepped down the stairs and saw Cadan standing with her parents, she rushed to his side. She was thinner, but her bright smile was unchanged. Her green eyes drew him in as she said with affection "Oh Cadan". It was obvious, the girl loved him deeply.

There was jubilation at the Wolf's dinner table that night. Lucy and Lily Ann prepared a fine dinner. Yet, they voiced concern for Cadan as he traveled alone in winter which could be quite dangerous. It was ironic that he made the trip when they were to move back to Credence in the spring. They insisted he stay with them sharing Harold's room rather than at a hotel which suited him fine. Copper was also sheltered in their small barn which sat behind their store. He could eat and rest for the trek back.

As the family chatted in the parlor, Cadan excused himself, went into Harold's room where his things were and removed Lily's Valentine present from the saddlebag. When he returned to the parlor, he placed the small package gently in her hands.

"What's this?" she asked.

"It's your Valentine present. I hope you like it," he said shyly.

Franz and Lucy watched quietly as they looked at

the young couple on their parlor settee. It pleased them knowing their daughter was being courted in such a loving manner. No doubt, they seemed destined for one another.

Harold, stopped looking out the main street window, shut the drape and joined the group. He sat down in a chair and had a curious look on his young face. He wondered what Cadan gave his sister.

When Lily Ann unwrapped the package and took out the music box she gasped. "Oh, how beautiful. I shall always treasure it."

Taking the key, he wound it and suddenly a tiny mechanical bird appeared, fluttered its wings, twisted its head back and forth and sang as if alive. It was magical for all of them.

That night while Franz, Lucy and Harold slept soundly, Lily Ann and Cadan tossed and turned knowing the other was just down the hall. Excited. their young hearts brimmed with love and desire. Neither of them could sleep a wink.

Part III

After a wonderful visit, it was time for him to return to Credence. Leaving at sunrise once again, he said goodbye to the girl he loved and her family and quietly rode out of the gulch. He passed both sleepy-eyed men on their way to their claims and others staggering from saloons after a night of dissipation.

He knew he would ask Franz for Lily Ann's hand in marriage once they moved back. There was much planning to do and decisions to make. First he needed to write his mother and Silas notifying him of his plans. How he wished they could meet her.

It was a calm morning and the sun shone brightly as it had three days prior. Their twelve-mile trip started out quiet and uneventful. Still, both he and Copper were constantly alert for what they might encounter.

A few hours later they came upon a large herd of gray-brown deer foraging in a draw. Birds chittered and flew in and out of the pines. The forest teemed with all manner of wildlife and he often felt eyes watching him as he and Copper traveled on. Now and then a pinecone dropped as the wind rustled through evergreen branches It was a stunningly beautiful place he felt. Suddenly, Copper's ears pricked up. Cadan wondered what caught his attention. Then he spotted a large bobcat standing boldly in the road glaring through startling yellow eyes as if demanding a toll. Copper stopped unsure of what the cat might do. Then it jumped effortlessly and disappeared over the embankment. It was a strange sight. Copper turned his handsome head around and looked at his rider. Cadan patted his powerful neck, assuring him all would be fine. Still, he felt there was no time to tarry. As the horse trotted down the road, Cadan was reassured once again his formidable weapons would protect him from harm.

Within a half hour from the settlement, clouds had completely shrouded the sun. Soon after, the temperature dropped dramatically and was accompanied by a fierce north wind. After all, it was February but being so close to Credence he felt there was no reason to worry. How foolish he was to think it would be an early spring he thought to himself. Calmly he unrolled his old wool coat and buttoned it up to his neck. Before he left that morning, Lily Ann gave him a rather long crochet muffler in two shades of blue. Her hands worked lovingly on it he could tell. She planned on giving the muffler to him when the family returned to Credence. He tied part of it around his head and neck and put the remaining portion inside his coat to keep his chest warm. Remembering his gloves, he dug into his pockets, found the left one, but the right was missing. He had no idea it fell into the bottom of the coat lining after he ripped the pocket on his way to Deadwood. It concerned him greatly as his hands were getting cold. He wished he had worn mittens instead.

Within ten minutes it began to snow heavily. It was rather light and resembled flour making it difficult to breathe because it was so fine. Rather than fall vertically from the sky it seemed to fly wildly in all directions, making their travel difficult. Copper remained on course focused on his cozy stall waiting for him and Jens who he loved. After only fifteen minutes his Cadan could not see through the blinding snow and wind. Small drifts grew into massive ones, still Copper navigated through the treacherous blizzard knowing they would perish if he failed.

Cadan struggled to secure the muffler around his face and head. He resembled a mummy with eyes hidden in the folds, often obscuring his view. Over and over he tried to keep his right hand warm by burrowing it in a pocket. But as his left hand tried to grip the reins, his right hand fought to keep the scarf wound his head and neck. He constantly shifted in the saddle attempting to buffet the blizzard winds, confusing Copper as to what his rider wanted him to do. Strange sensations in his right hand felt like needles. He began to panic when it became numb and he burrowed it once more in his coat pocket. The glove on his left hand was no longer able to keep it warm and he fumbled with the reins. They slipped from his fingers and lashed into Copper's face spooking him. He jumped back jostling his rider. Since Cadan's clothing was frozen to the saddle, it kept him from falling to the ground. Copper quickly regained his senses, put his head down and continued like a battleship caught in raging seas.

By now it was bitterly cold. The ferocious wind sliced through Cadan's clothing. Their progress was slowed down considerably by the monster storm. He couldn't stop shivering. One by one thoughts of his loved ones flashed through his brain. He sensed he was about to die on the frozen mountain far from his homeland. Then his mother's soothing voice came to him saying, *"Cadan means 'battle', my son,"* before he drifted off.

Jens was shutting the livery door when he noticed a lone horse walking through the blizzard with a rider slumped in the saddle.

"No, I can't believe it. You damn fool!" Jens took off through the snow and wind shouting, "Help! Help! I need help!"

Henry happened to be looking out the window when he saw Jens running and shouting. Immediately, Henry, Ginger and a few others that were waiting out the storm in the Nugget, ran outside to see what was wrong. They were shocked to see Cadan and Copper in the middle of the road heavily coated with snow and ice. Henry and Ginger quickly took Cadan to Jacob's office wondering if he was still alive while Jens led Copper to a warm, safe stall.

While carrying his friend, Ginger kept saying, "Jesus,

Mary and Joseph!" while Henry muttered something to himself.

When Dr McIntosh saw Cadan his face turned grave. "Hurry! We must get him out of this clothing and place him under warm blankets!"

It seemed weather had proven the most dangerous foe on Cadan's journey, not animals or mankind after all.

Part IV

Within days, painful blisters appeared on Cadan's right hand. Some of his fingers turned an ugly purplish-black, an indication of irreversible damage to tissue and blood flow. Gangrene would have set in if Jacob hadn't amputated the ring and little finger on his right hand. It was necessary in order to keep the infection from spreading. Jacob, was not a "Saw Bones" but a skilled surgeon. He witnessed more soldiers die of infections than battle wounds. The loss of his fingers was more important than the loss of his life. With each passing day, Cadan's healing progressed. It was a long horrible process and he was very ill for weeks. Furthermore, his emotions were ravaged and that was something no medicine nor caring physician could cure.

It was a hideous thing for Cadan to endure and the pain was unbearable. He suffered greatly. Dr. McIntosh changed the bandages each day checking for signs of infection which could easily happen if not for his attention to cleanliness. It was a miracle no more damage occurred. If not for the thick, crochet scarf, parts of his face, nose and ears would have been disfigured. There was little doubt he would have lost his life if not for Copper. Still, rather than feel gratitude for his life, he fell into a depression and self-loathing.

"I should have listened and not traveled alone. Why did I travel in winter anyway? I'm such a stupid fool. Lily Ann probably doesn't love me anyway. What if I hadn't stuffed the gloves in the coat so hard? Why didn't I take mittens instead of gloves they would have kept my hands safe? Why did I come here? I never belonged here in the first place. I will never play the piano again. I'm cursed".

He mourned the loss of his fingers. His nights were often filled with hideous, bizarre nightmares of pianos, black and white keys blurred together and fingerless, bleeding hands. Other times he would be playing beautifully and wake only to discover bandages. He still felt them, but they were gone, replaced by phantom fingers that served to remind him of what the storm stole. Dr. McIntosh tried to reassure him how miraculous it was to be alive and mending. But he did not agree, thinking the doctor was in too much of a hurry in amputating. Cadan always spoke through the piano. He defined himself with his music and it was an extension of himself. Without it, he felt lost. He vacillated between grief and rage. He refused to even look at his beloved piano thinking he could no longer play. Finally, he became withdrawn.

One Sunday afternoon he heard a knock on his door, opened it a crack and saw the smiling faces of his friends, Ginger and Denis. As they stepped closer they could see his little cabin was a mess and smelled stuffy.

"Would you like to come in?" Cadan asked quietly.

"No, it's too fine a day to sit inside. Let's enjoy the sun on our faces," Denis said with a little laugh.

Ginger pushed past Cadan, picked up a small hand-hewn table and put it behind the cabin. Then he came back and picked up a couple of rustic log chairs.

"Get another one for me Cadan," he ordered pointing to a remaining one.

Placing them around the table he motioned to Cadan. "Let's eat!"

Denis placed the basket in the middle of the table. As Denis opened it they were met by an amazing aroma. The basket contained Klara's roast beef and vegetable stew, baked bread, and apple pie. She thoughtfully packed plates, napkins, utensils and three tin cups.

"You always enjoyed Klara's cooking. Her feelings are hurt that you don't eat with us anymore. She thinks you don't like her cooking," Denis said with a smile.

Ginger pulled the cork from the whiskey, took a swig for himself and poured substantial amounts into the cups.

"To your health my Cornish friend," he said in his rich brogue.

Cadan remained silent. They noticed his eyes well with tears. Then, taking the cup in his left hand took a long sip, then another. His face regained some color and finally a little smile appeared. The three men ate, drank and visited for hours, sharing stories of their life some quite painful, others filled with mirth. It was healing for all of them. Ginger had an idea to throw a party for Copper at the Nugget as he was considered the town hero. Cadan's eyebrows went up and Denis chuckled. "And why not? He is a noble steed and warrior. Jens would agree. Horses enjoy beer like the rest of us. Besides, he smells far better than most of the patrons in the Nugget anyhow," he said with seriousness. The three men laughed at the thought of the big sorrel standing in the saloon slurping beer.

They talked of many things from religion to politics, their differences as well as similarities. Finally, they spoke of the families they left behind. Denis never discussed the tragic loss of his first wife and son to anyone except Klara until that moment. Both Ginger and Cadan were shocked knowing what Denis went through.

Ginger shared the story of his family's famine years and how much they suffered in Ireland, his voice shaking at times. Hunger, deprivation, despair, and anguish were no strangers to the Fitzgerald family.

Looking at Cadan he said "If you live long enough my friend, you will suffer and face many losses. But you don't need to endure it alone. Look around, you're not alone."

As promised, in the first week of May, the Wolf family returned. Instead of Cadan greeting them, Henry did. Henry had written Franz a letter explaining what took place on Cadan's return trip. Lily Ann was distraught, yet relieved and thankful he was alive. She understood why he hadn't written her with his severely injured hand. But she didn't understand why he wasn't there to meet them now that they were home.

As soon as she got down from the wagon, she half walked, half ran to his tiny cabin. She knocked on his door and called out his name. Her parents had much unpacking to do and moving of furniture. Harold was put to work which kept him from spying on his sister.

Lily Ann stood by the cabin door for a few minutes. She heard movement inside. It confused her why he wouldn't answer. After a few minutes, the door slowly opened.

He was thin and his warm brown eyes looked sad. He quickly crossed his arms, hiding his right hand from her view.

"Hello Lily Ann, it's good to see you," he said quietly.

"Cadan, oh how I have missed you," she said in a soft and tender voice.

As soon as she spoke the words, he stepped outside and embraced her saying, "I love you."

She looked up to him, touched his face gently and answered, "I love you too and always will."

"I've been meaning to write you but couldn't. Things just aren't the same anymore. Do you understand what I mean?" he said slowly.

"No, I don't understand. I love you and you love me. That's all I know and that's all that matters. Besides, you promised to teach me how to play the piano! I heard you could play with one hand and drink with the other," she replied with frustration rising in her voice.

Her words stung him. They were unexpected and cruel, he felt.

"Why would you say such things, knowing what I have lost?" he said in a hesitant, choked voice.

"All I know is you are standing in front of me making excuses. You and I are going to sit down at your piano and play. I've waited a year for you to be by my side. I'm not waiting any longer!" she spoke impatiently.

"You know I can't play anymore. Why are you saying these things to me, Lily Ann? You just told me you loved me!" he replied with anger.

"It's because I love you that I'm saying these things.

You will play again, only differently, just as you will teach me how to play. You seem to have forgotten the challenges you've already overcome. Traveling all the way to America alone through wild country, filing your claim, working it, selling it, building a life of your own here proved your courage. You are more than a gifted pianist. You are the man I have fallen deeply in love with, a friend to many and a son your parents surely are proud of."

He stood quietly, listening to the auburn-haired girl with the bright smile. He finally realized he truly was a blessed man for he found love and valuable friends.

He recalled the trials his mother, Gwenna, endured. She had shown strength, faith and determination throughout her life. Suddenly he was ashamed of his self-pity. Two years ago, he set out to find himself, test himself, and be his own man and he had done just that. Now, standing before him, was his future.

That evening Franz locked the store, pulled down the shades and put the closed sign on the door. Everyone was weary from the move. They quietly went upstairs except for Lily Ann who sat with Cadan at his piano.

She watched as he put his left hand on the keys but hesitated with the right. Gently, she took his scarred, maimed right hand, placed it on the keys next to her left hand, looked at him and said,

"Now my dear, it looks like we will be playing duets from now on. Shall we begin?"

♬ ♪ ♫

Saturday
December 22, 1877

Some guests stood on the steps with the door ajar, allowing fresh air to flow in and out. With so many people, it would have grown too warm and close if everyone squeezed inside.

The room glowed with soft candlelight making it appear other worldly. Likewise, the store counter had been transformed with a long white tablecloth festooned with garlands of pine and ribbons. It held a splendid feast. A tall evergreen stood next to the piano filling the room with its scent. It held glittering glass ornaments from Germany as well as homemade.

At the request of the bride and groom, special guests sat in front. They held fiddles, concertinas and flutes. To the astonishment of everyone, Ginger shaved his long, unruly hair and straggly beard making him look at least twenty years younger. Scrubbed, polished and dressed fashionably, he looked quite dashing. For that matter, miners who usually neglected their appearance showed up bathed, shaved and wearing their finest clothing.

Denis, Klara and little Sofia sat in front as did Jacob McIntosh, Jens and his wife, Henry and Stephen. Denis was especially attentive to Klara as they were expecting a child in the spring.

Lucy drew admiring glances as she smiled and greeted guests. They had never seen her look so lovely. She wore a sapphire blue silk taffeta gown with matching sapphire drop earrings. Her face, slightly flushed, gave her a girlish look.

Across the room, Franz tapped his feet nervously at the bottom of the staircase. When Lily Ann appeared, a brief fiddle rendition of Mendelssohn's Wedding March signaled guests to stand. Harold proudly escorted his sister down the stairs to her father's awaiting arm.

All eyes focused on the bride as she made her entrance. She wore a lavish gown of ivory silk embellished with cream-colored lace with pearls on the sleeves, hem and neckline. Her full length ivory colored lace veil was exquisite. It was fastened to her auburn tresses which she wore softly up secured with seed pearl hair pins. She was stunningly beautiful and reminiscent of a fairytale princess.

The groom was handsome in his starched, white dress shirt, black suit and vest with gold pocket watch. When Lily Ann stood by his side he whispered, "You take my breath away."

Before they spoke their vows , they recited one line from a favorite poem written by Christopher Marlowe in 1599 titled: "The Passionate Shepherd to His Love"

"Come live with me and be my love"...

The ceremony was simple and brief. Lily Ann's thick wedding band was made from gold taken from Cadan's placer mine and inscribed with their wedding date, 12-22-77, initials C.G. & L.G. with the word, FOREVER. When the minister announced them man and wife, Cadan kissed his bride passionately, raising some eyebrows.

Standing hand in hand, Cadan looked out at their guests and said, "My wife and I have a gift for you."

Then stepping over to the piano they sat down and began playing a duet, "Silent Night."

Cadan and Lily Ann were as one, hitting each note with feeling and perfection. Many were moved to tears for they did not expect to hear him play ever again. They were witnessing a tender moment and a miracle of sorts. Over the months, Cadan developed his own style enabling his right hand to play without the missing fingers. The technique was often painful, demanding practice and patience.

The young couple chose *Silent Night* as it was perfect for the evening. Some guests sang the lyrics making it more special. Cadan and Lily Ann would play many duets throughout their life but mostly private ones.

It was still and quiet that December evening. Fluffy snow fell gently for a few minutes coating everything in soft white. As the clouds drifted away, a full moon and stars appeared and the snow sparkled and shimmered like magic.

When they stopped playing, everyone was left spellbound. Then the room erupted in applause and cheers.

Franz, Lucy and Harold rushed over and hugged them. Laughing, Franz, turned to the crowd and said, "It's time to eat! Come, help yourselves my friends! There is enough for everyone." It was true. Nobody that evening would leave hungry, thirsty or unhappy.

"Before we make merry, let me toast the bride and groom!" Ginger shouted in a jubilant voice.

"What's your pleasure sir?" Franz asked Ginger.

"A glass of beer will do," he replied.

Franz quickly filled a tall glass with beer and handed it to him. Lifting the glass Ginger spoke clearly,

"I wish you and your beautiful bride good health, wealth and God willing, a house full of children, To never ending blessings and happiness Cadan and Lily Ann!"

Cadan went to Ginger and hugged him tightly. The little Irishman was his best friend.

The room filled with laughter, feasting and music.

— Menu —

Wild Turkey, Deer, Elk, Roast Chicken, Ham Oysters & Fish
Stewed Carrots, Squash, and Roasted Potatoes
Rolls and Mounds of Butter
Plum and Apple Jelly
Plum Pudding
Assorted Pies
Vienna Chocolate
Peppermints
Hickory Nut and Almond Macaroons
Caramels
Wedding Cake
Beer, Whiskey, Wine, Coffee, Milk and Sarsaparilla

Lily Ann requested "Joy to the World," to be sung by Denis Moreau because as it was the happiest moment in her life.

Cadan had a surprise waiting for her, but it would have to wait until most of their wedding guests were gone so they could finally slip away. She had no idea that weeks prior to their marriage, Lucy, Franz and Cadan turned his rudimentary cabin into a charming and sweet cottage. It was not easy keeping Lily Ann away. Nevertheless, they succeeded. The small dwelling now held a magnificent brass bed and was fitted with soft cotton sheets, fluffy pillows and a gorgeous rose- colored satin quilt that resembled a cloud. A small dressing table sat along one wall while a beautiful wardrobe with beveled mirror nestled on another. A bottle of champagne with two goblets waited on top of a tiny oak table that came with two matching chairs. Cheerful woven drapes hung on the windows, keeping cold drafts out and privacy in. A pretty set of dishes sat on the shelves of a quaint cupboard with napkins and linens already placed in the drawers. Shiny new pots, pans and utensils hung above the stove and the rough- hewn wooden plank floor was completely covered with heavy wool rugs. The dark little cabin was now a home filled with brightness and beauty.

Wedding gifts were placed under the tree and spilled on top of the piano. Some were wrapped in brown paper tied by twine. Jens gave the couple a large, heavy hammer that Thor would have been proud to hold. It symbolized building a new life together. A few guests ordered things from mail order catalogs, many gifts were tiny nuggets of gold and nestled in small draw string bags or pouches.

As Cadan glanced at faces in the room, he felt a deep joy but a tinge of sadness too. The faces he wished to see most were absent. It was impossible for them to attend given the harsh winter and deep snows that soon would arrive.

With no railroad, traveling in and out was dangerous if not impossible. They sent a long letter along with a monetary gift. Yet, the gift that meant more to him than anything was reading his parents were coming to Credence in the spring.

♫ ♪ ♬

A Stagecoach to Credence

Crawling over steep hills and pitted roads, the stage carried its passengers through harsh terrain where rail lines had not yet been established. The constant jostling up and down and rocking back and forth could leave passengers with bumps and bruises. It was not a comfortable nor tranquil mode of transportation, but its inhabitants did not complain. They were enjoying the adventure of it all.

It was not fitted as a treasure coach; therefore, it did not attract road agents. On a May day in 1878, it carried four passengers, an elegant middle-age English couple and two shotgun messengers carrying sawn-off double-barreled shotguns loaded with buckshot.

The male passenger, Silas Gray reflected on his life as the coach rambled on. Though he came from a family of means, much of it was lost due to the mindless pursuits of his parents and older brother who perished in a shipwreck while he was away at school. Essentially, there was little of the estate remaining, but he managed to salvage some of it. The only sensible thing his parents ever did was send him to a fine school where he excelled in economics. He was a man to reckon with no doubt.

He wore spectacles tinted blue to shade his hazel eyes. Now at fifty-three, his once coal black hair was streaked with gray adding to his distinction. As he kept his own counsel, he was dubbed by many, the mysterious Mr. Gray.

Skilled in all manner of weaponry and an expert marksman, he nevertheless hired the shotgun messengers for their journey west. Silas never left anything to chance.

He gazed at his wife of twenty-six years and thought her lovely. She was unusually quiet as they drew closer to their destination. He wondered what she was thinking while she stared out the stage window. It had been three years since Cadan traveled to America. They corresponded through letters, but it wasn't the same. Silas reached over, took her small hand and squeezed it. She moved closer and put her head on his shoulder. She adored him.

Silas and Gwenna had shared much together. He recalled his joy at finding her with the Romani people. If not for their kindness and generosity, she and her unborn baby would have likely perished. They sheltered her as one does a lost child. They understood what it meant to be unwelcome and misunderstood. Silas discovered her sitting in their camp with a huge multi-colored dog sleeping by her feet.

"Gwenna!" he shouted. She looked up from her needlework and noticed Silas running towards her.

She stood up, dropping her embroidery in the grass. As Silas approached, Patch let out a low growl and placed himself directly in front of her, shielding her. She stroked his massive head saying, "Shhh boy, it's fine."

She began to tremble and tears welled up at the sight of him.

"Gwenna, I have been searching for weeks. Are you alright? I have been so worried," he said in earnest.

The scene held a little crowd spellbound. It was not often a fine carriage carrying such a gentleman was in their midst and they found it all quite romantic.

He tenderly wrapped his arms around her. "My Gwenna, my love. Nobody will ever harm you again. I promise."

Silas thanked Andrei and Esmerelda. He also gave them an enormous sum for protecting her. He would never forget their goodness and promised them they would never want for anything the rest of their lives.

Esmerelda hugged Gwenna goodbye, handed her the needlework she dropped in the grass and said, "May each of your days be stitched with threads of love."

The carriage took off with its passengers when they noticed Patch running alongside the wheels barking frantically.

"What's this? Stop the carriage. I don't want the dog to be injured," Silas shouted to the driver.

"He has not left my side since they found me," she replied.

When the carriage halted. Someone in the crowd yelled, "The dog belongs with her!"

Silas and Patch looked at one another. Shrugging, he opened the door and Patch jumped inside.

Shaking his head he said, "Well, I trust everyone is comfortable?"

Patch was not the only one who belonged with her.

That same day Silas proposed. They married hurriedly and discreetly, with few guests present.

A lifetime ago, he mused to himself, as they drew closer to their destination.

Part II

When the stage pulled into Credence a young couple stood on the porch of Wolf's Dry Goods. The auburn-haired girl looked radiant, the young man strong and proud.

Before the coach halted, Cadan was on the street with Lily Ann close behind. Franz, Lucy and Harold came out of the store and politely waited under the overhang. Henry and Stephen stood outside the Nugget. Jens, always met the stage, but this time stopped and watched. He realized it was a special moment and didn't wish to interrupt.

Before the driver climbed down from his seat, Cadan swung the coach door open saying,

"Mother, father, welcome!"

Silas jumped out of the coach first and gallantly helped his wife down while the two shotgun messengers headed for the Nugget. They wanted to quench their thirst.

Cadan was struck by how fit and handsome his father was. It cheered him to see how little his mother had changed too. Her warm brown eyes with gold specks were still bright as ever and her dark brown hair held a few gray strands although she had gained a little weight.

Mother and son embraced for a long time. Gwenna, was overwhelmed and dabbed her eyes now and then with her lace hankie. Silas, showing more reserve, shook hands and then hugged Cadan.

"Lily Ann! Come meet my parents!" Cadan said to his wife, who shyly stood a few paces away. Lily Ann wore her hair up, held only by a silk ribbon that matched her soft-hued green cotton dress. She looked like a spring day, fresh and sweet

As Gwenna looked lovingly at her son, she realized he was a self-assured, courageous man. It pained her mother's heart to see his scarred hand with its missing fingers. She had always been fiercely protective of him. She knew the right time would come for him to share his ordeal; however, she still wanted to hold his hand as she once did when he was a little boy.

Looking at him she realized he was no longer a child but a husband and one day maybe even a father. She was pleased to witness the devotion between her son and Lily Ann. She sensed they were meant for one another just as she and Silas were. Gwenna noticed he still stuttered somewhat and thought some things would always remain the same. He was her only child and it broke her heart when he left. She and Silas were unable to have children of their own. Although it pained them, they accepted it as they did with other obstacles they encountered. Silas gave her more than she could have ever imagined. Although he couldn't protect her from certain things like gossip or envy, their love was built on solid ground from which they drew joy and strength.

"Let's get you off the street and settled first, Mother. You must be exhausted. You will be staying in a boarding house run by friends of ours, Denis and Klara. I think you will like it very much. She's a fine good cook and Denis is quite an interesting fellow," Cadan said.

"Yes, we must get out of these dusters," Gwenna agreed, while brushing the fine road dust from herself. "We found traveling by stage is not only hazardous but dirty," she answered.

"Harold and I will help with your luggage," Franz insisted.

Franz was very impressed with the stylish couple the moment they stepped of the stage. Lucy just smiled and said hello. There would be plenty of time to become acquainted since they would be staying for a month. She sensed their visit would hold great meaning not only for her son-in law, but her daughter too.

Lucy's premonition was right. For Cadan didn't realize his parents brought two very special wedding gifts from his late grandfather, Charles.

Dinner at the Denis and Klara's boarding house was very special that evening. Klara's meal was far better than any Gwenna and Silas had tasted since they left England. They appreciated the hearty meal and exceedingly clean accommodations. Klara and Denis created a beautiful little hotel. Lily Ann baked two fruit pies for the occasion hoping to impress her new in-laws. She wanted them to know Cadan was well cared for. The evening was filled with warmth and convivial conversation. After a while, Silas looked at Gwenna and said, "Perhaps it's time we give them the wedding presents from Charles."

"I can't think of a better moment," Gwenna replied with excitement.

"Wedding presents from Sir Charles? I'm amazed. How very kind of him. I know he was ill at the time of our wedding and to think of us. I wish you could have met him Lily Ann." Cadan said with sincerity.

Reaching into his lapel, Silas removed a small black velvet box and a waxed sealed envelope. Handing the small box to Cadan he said, "This belonged to your grandmother, Lady Eliot. It was her engagement ring. Charles felt it should be on your wife's finger," Silas said.

Cadan opened the box where a 1.30 carat Columbian emerald with two matching 1.10 carat white diamonds glistened. The young couple gasped. The ring was incredible.

"Put it on," Cadan said.

"How very beautiful! But,I will never take my wedding band off, even for this," Lily said.

Taking her right hand, he placed it on her ring finger. It fit perfectly.

"Now, it's where it belongs," Gwenna said cheerfully to her daughter in-law.

Lily Ann, stared at the ring, looked at Cadan, then back to Gwenna and Silas. She was stunned. "I can't wait to show my parents. Whatever will they say? I don't know what to say. I shall never forget this moment," she said softly.

Gwenna's tone changed and became more serious, "Son, there is much more. Please listen."

Silas began, "This envelope contains a letter written by Charles before he died along with his will. The letter is personal and meant for only you to read. The will was drawn up shortly before he died. It's legal and binding.

"Son, your grandfather left his entire estate to you which includes land, farms, and business holdings. You were his only blood heir and he loved you. You now hold his title."

Cadan looked at his mother and back to Silas without saying a word. His face was expressionless. He felt for sure he hadn't heard him correctly. In a moment he said, "What? I don't think I understand. "

"I think your grandfather left you his house and belongings," Lily Ann said to her husband innocently. For she had no concept of what her husband had inherited.

Gwenna spoke up, "Son, Charles left you everything. We felt you should hear it from us and not in a letter. Glencove is your home. You are needed there. We need you there. Silas and I had no idea Charles had such plans for you."

Cadan sat quietly while Lily Ann stared at the ring which now sat on her finger. It was incomprehensible to think he was left Glencove knowing the circumstances that surrounded his birth. Now, it became clear to him that his aristocratic grandfather had been watching him since the time he was born, following his every move and loving him without saying. Cadan had planned on returning home before too long anyway. But now he would be returning sooner and with his wife.

He said, "Our children will love growing up there just as I did. We'll leave the first part of August if it's fine with you, that way she will have a little more time with her family."

"There's more than enough room for her family too," Gwenna laughed softly. "Glencove is massive." Hearing that, Lily Ann sighed a breath of relief for she knew her parents would take it hard to see her go far from their protective arms.

The month in Credence was spent meeting Cadan's

good friends which included Copper. Jens laughed as she fed the horse carrots saying, "You are a noble steed, Sir Copper, and we are here to reward you." Silas and Gwenna truly were indebted to the horse for saving their son and paid Jens a king's ransom. "If only I could take him back home and spoil him," she sighed.

Cadan took his parents to the claim he once worked and demonstrated the process of placer mining. They were fascinated by everything he showed them. Some of the Cornish miners reminded Gwenna of her brothers back home and it surprised her how many were working and living there.

Gwenna and Silas were impressed with the tidy log cabin he built for himself. However, more than anything, they were amazed at his courage. He had traveled far, worked hard and underwent many changes since coming to the territory.

It was a wilderness and nothing like his upbringing. The native culture and history of the place interested Silas, but made Gwenna uneasy. She felt the area was rife with danger overall, though it was ruggedly beautiful. They realized how hard everyone worked to build a new life and home for themselves in Credence and they wished them well.

Gwenna enjoyed visiting Lucy and Klara. They sensed the hardships they had all endured and shared a few stories of survival. Gwenna appreciated the wild beauty of the hills, its wildflowers and wild creatures. She talked endlessly about the flowers she nurtured at Glencove, her brothers, William and James, and a little about her life before she became Mrs. Gray.

It was the first week of June and time for Silas and Gwenna to return to Cornwall. They shook hands with their new friends, kissed Cadan and Lily Ann goodbye and boarded the stage along with the two shotgun messengers.

The following months Cadan and Lily Ann spent planning their new life together. Change was exciting and daunting for Lily Ann. Still, she had confidence in not only Cadan, but herself. Cadan had his father to help him with his new role and he was excited to begin. Before they left, Silas and Gwenna asked Franz and Lucy if they would consider moving to Glencove. It was a huge decision, but Franz would be closer to his homeland and Lily Ann and Lucy would have each other. Harold was excited and thought it would be an adventure.

Cadan's friends were sad to see him leave. They sat in The Nugget one evening and talked of their futures.

"I am selling my mines and going back to Ireland. I haven't seen my dear mother and sister for years. I miss them. Besides, I want to find a bride of my own before I'm too old and ugly!" Ginger said laughing.

It was true. Thomas Fitzgerald had stored enough money to live comfortably the rest of his life. Ireland beckoned him home. He wanted to leave as soon as possible for he sensed change in the air.

"Well, that means we will see each other often my Irish friend. I will have to introduce you to my uncles, William and James. They were hard working miners, just as my mother had been a maid. There are no pretenses in my family, nor will there ever be. Come let's toast to our futures," he said heartily.

"Would you play a song on the old piano one last time?"

Henry said from behind the bar.

"It won't be the same without you," Stephen said, emotion in his voice. He rarely spoke making everyone in the room fall silent.

"Why not! I'll do my best but remember, a part of me is missing, but a part of me will remain," Cadan answered.

"Is that some kind of riddle?" Denis asked.

"No, it's the truth. I will always be a part of this place just as everyone here is," Cadan said, his tone sounding strange and melancholy.

He played a last song on the battered piano that evening for his friends and it never sounded better.

The goodbyes were bittersweet for it meant never seeing Denis Moreau again, nor Jacob McIntosh, Jens, Henry or woeful Stephen. The distance was too great. He needed to say goodbye to another dear friend, Copper.

When Cadan opened the livery door, Copper nickered a greeting. The horse sensed it was goodbye. They were alone. Taking his huge head in his hands and looking into his eyes, Cadan spoke, "Thank you boy. I shall miss you."

Cadan noticed Copper had gray and white hairs on his coat and muzzle. He looked much older. Their dangerous trek from Deadwood had aged him considerably — there would be no more long trails for the big sorrel. The rest of his life would be spent in grazing and comfort. Cadan kissed him on his forehead, stroked his soft neck and mane, and walked out the door, tears streaming down his face.

He played on his beautiful piano each day and night before they left. Sometimes Lily Ann and Cadan practiced sweet duets for her parents and brother. Usually, he played alone and with great feeling and emotion. The piano was more than an instrument, it had shared his experiences and those of others.

Before the young couple embarked on their new life, he gifted his remarkable and beloved piano to Franz and Lucy, feeling it would remain cherished and safe. Franz stated he would not leave America so Cadan felt they would always have it. Franz came from Germany to build a better life which he did. However, as the weeks sped by, Franz dwelled on his decision to stay in Credence rather than leave for England. He loved his business and it thrived. Yet, he was wise and saw gold mining towns go bust. His instincts told him it would eventually take place in Credence. Not only that, both he and Lucy missed their daughter. Lily Ann wrote about her wonderful new life, but she longed for her family.

Two years later, Franz stood on a ladder and removed his Wolf's Dry Goods sign. He placed it in the back of the freight wagon with their belongings, furniture and heirlooms. The Wolf family were sailing for Cornwall England to be near their daughter, son-in-law and baby grandson, Gawain. A new owner would soon take over, changing the name of the store but Franz felt the piano belonged with Henry instead. Henry was Cadan's friend and would appreciate having the piano far more. He could tinkle the keys now and then if he wished. The Nugget's old and battered saloon piano was damaged and broken and long since gone. Now, the magnificent one would grace the building. And so, with great effort and care, the piano was relocated across the street into The Nugget's storeroom, safe and dry.

As Franz had predicted, gold mining eventually ceased

in Credence. The miners left one by one, seeking their fortunes in other mines across the west. Denis, Klara, Sofia and their baby boy, Jacques moved back to northern Minnesota where he had family. Stephen died and was buried nearby. The banker moved to a community east of the Missouri. The minister and his wife left for Nebraska and Dr. McIntosh set up practice in Denver. Jens and his wife moved twelve miles away to Deadwood. He opened another livery stable only without noble Copper who was buried in the back of the Credence livery.

Henry found himself alone. Every building in Credence was vacant, except for his. He wondered why some structures were left with doors ajar or windows open as though their owners would soon return. But, they never would.

He looked around the saloon that had been his life. It was empty. For a second he heard the voices of his friends laughing, but it soon vanished. He walked outside, looked around and found the street deserted. Even the stray cats that for years found refuge with him had disappeared. He felt hollow. Then he put all the tables and chairs in order, washed glasses, shined the mirror behind the bar and dusted lamps and fixtures. Upstairs he straightened up the rooms where travelers slept, closed their drapes and shut their doors one last time.

His heart shattered. He was a broken man as he boarded up the front door and windows of the Nugget. He kept looking down the street as if a stage or wagon train would soon arrive carrying loads of excited passengers full of dreams. But no stage or wagon train pulled up.

Finished, he went back to the storage room to gather

his belongings and say goodbye to all he loved. "It looks like we both have been forgotten my friend," he said quietly to the piano.

He touched it lovingly for it brought only the happiest memories. Henry stepped outside and boarded the back window and door of the storage room. When he was satisfied everything was secure, he placed the hammer and nails next to a tree behind the building. He stood alone for a moment staring into the distance, then picked up his bags and walked away never to be seen or heard from again.

Abandoned and vulnerable, the houses, cabins, shanties and buildings fell victim one by one to the elements. Yet, for some unknown reason, The Nugget and its lone survivor remained for the most part, untouched.

♬ ♫ ♫

Star Dust & Moonbeams

Mark watched the alarm clock tick away. It was two-thirty a.m. and he couldn't fall back to sleep after having a strange dream. It struck him as real and he couldn't seem to shake it. So, he decided to get up for a sip of water and check on the kids. He carefully crawled out of bed so Elizabeth wouldn't be disturbed, put on his robe and tip-toed up the stairs to their rooms. He found them fast asleep and tucked them in before heading back down the stairs and into the kitchen.

It was a warm August evening with a gentle breeze. The heavens were filled with endless constellations flooding the backyard with an ethereal glow. As he sipped the cool water, he thought of his busy day ahead and the flooding of the old mining town of Credence. Everything will vanish as if it never existed, he thought to himself. Suddenly, a little moonbeam hovered in the air, touched a wall and countertop before settling on the floor where it shimmered back and forth. He was mesmerized for a few minutes. It's only a bit of glittering star dust he reasoned with himself— gold dust of sorts. But he wondered about the coincidence of the date, August 15th, the same day the piano arrived in

Credence back in 1875.

When the moon beam disappeared, he put the water glass in the sink, peeked out the window and noticed the garage light was still on. That's odd. I could have sworn I turned it off before going to bed, he thought shaking his head. When he opened the door he glanced at the fine old piano sitting majestically against the wall and said in a low voice, "I'm glad I found you and brought you home."

Then he reached up, pulled the string to turn off the light, closed the door and shuffled back to bed were he immediately drifted off.

At breakfast the next morning Elizabeth noticed him yawning and rubbing his eyes.

"It looks like I'm not the only one who didn't get much sleep," she said.

"I'm sorry honey. Did I wake you?" Mark asked.

"No, it wasn't you. It was just one of those nights. At least it didn't take me too long to fall back to sleep," she answered.

"Wow! I sure had a restless night. Maybe it was the long day at the site or excitement of bringing the old piano home. I'm not sure. My dreams were so real I couldn't get back to sleep. So, I got up, checked the kids and got a drink of water. You should have seen the early morning sky! It was magical! We even had our very own little moonbeam right here in the kitchen. No wonder I'm beat. Hey, I could have sworn I turned the light off in the garage last night. I must have forgotten, because it was still on," Mark said while relishing his last morsels of bacon and eggs.

"How can that be possible? While you were in the shower, I went back to the garage to check if you had turned them off and they were. The chain is far too high for the kids to reach, so how in the world...?" she answered.

Elizabeth sat quietly listening to him and asked, "Do you remember what your dream was about?"

"Yes, it was kind of weird. I thought I heard the piano playing a tune and it seemed so real that it woke me," he answered.

Elizabeth got up from the table, poured another cup of coffee, looked out the kitchen window at their children playing in the yard and sat back down.

With an astonished look on her face she whispered, "It seems we had the same dream. It was the faint tinkling of a piano playing that woke me too."

♬ ♫ ♪

About the Author

Carol Blackford is also the author of Grateful Heart, A True Story of Faith, Hope and Love, Under the Cottonwood, and Casey: A Firefighter's Story.

A Sioux Falls native, she always wanted to teach. Her first calling was to become a Kindergarten teacher, but instead taught 9-12 high school English. However, that was not to last. In 1981 she found herself teaching college English for South Dakota State University as well as other area colleges and universities. Now retired, Carol spends much of her time writing. She shares her life with her husband Terry and beloved horse, Traveler.

Carol can be reached at:
travthepaint@gmail.com

Other books by Carol Blackford

Carol Blackford's first book, **Grateful Heart: A True Story of Faith, Hope and Love,** was published in 2015. It has earned high praise from readers on Amazon and Goodreads.

> *"She is an impeccable wordsmith.*
> *Ms. Blackford provides a gentle road map."*

> *"Divine interventions do exist!*
> *I can't wait for the next Carol Blackford book!"*

> *"If everyone could have their story told like this."*

Carol's second book, **Under the Cottonwood,** was published in 2016.

> *"I have never read a book that made me laugh and cry so much."*

> *"Thank you for an excellent book Carol.*
> *I'm looking forward to reading your next one!"*

A third book, **Casey: A Firefighter's Story,** was published in 2018.

> *"Being a firefighter, this book really describes what we as 1st responders go through and our family. I would recommend this to anybody."*

Grateful Heart, Under the Cottonwood and **Casey: A Firefighter's Story** are available in select bookstores, as well as Amazon and Goodreads stores online.